Bristol Short Story Prize Anthology

Volume Ten

Bristol Short Story Prize Anthology Volume 10

First published 2017 by Tangent Books

Tangent Books
Unit 5.16 Paintworks
Bristol
BS4 3EH
0117 972 0645
www.tangentbooks.co.uk

Email: richard@tangentbooks.co.uk

ISBN: 9781910089651

Cover designed by Harry Sussams
www.harrysussams.com

Layout designed by Dave Oakley, Arnos Design
www.arnosdesign.co.uk

Printed and bound by ScandinavianBook.co.uk

A CIP catalogue record for this book is available from the British Library
www.tangentbooks.co.uk
www.bristolprize.co.uk

Contents

Introduction

A warm welcome to the 10ᵗʰ Bristol Short Story Prize Anthology. We're thrilled to be introducing 20 exceptional short stories, stories which we feel so fortunate to be publishing and which mark a decade of this competition.

This anthology is the result of hundreds of hours of graft, dedication and commitment mainly, of course, by the writers of the stories but also by all those involved in the Bristol Short Story Prize, especially our brilliant team of readers. They dived into their reading of the 2,000 entries and trimmed them down to a longlist of 40 with great enthusiasm and care. The longlist was then handed over to our panel of judges who were tasked with selecting 20 stories for this collection and from those 20, the top three winners.

The judging panel, chaired by short story maestro Tania Hershman, who was accompanied by writer Roshi Fernando, bookseller Simon Key, and literary agent, Juliet Pickering, discussed, debated, enthused and made crucial decisions with such unwaveringly forensic eyes and ears, and respect for each other's opinions. Different judges had different readings of the same story and it was fascinating listening in on the varied interpretations.

As Tania points out there were no easy decisions: "Wrangling with 40 stories in an attempt to shear off 20, then whittle down to the top 3, is a task that requires patience, openness, coffee, discussion, silence, and many piles of paper spread all over a large table. Speaking as someone who is honoured to be one of the judges for the fourth time, I think this year's BSSP longlist was the most diverse we've encountered – in terms of style and content, of humour and seriousness, of genres."

This year's entries did indeed cover a huge range of themes, however family, childhood, identity, migration and home kept appearing. There were far fewer dystopian stories than we have read in the past three or four years; perhaps the fractured, extreme state of recent worldwide political events have influenced that.

Thank you to Tania, Juliet, Roshi and Simon for selecting such a wonderful shortlist for this collection.

In the end they were left with four stories for the top three prizes. It was unanimously agreed that two stories should share the third prize - Bunmi Ogunsiji's wonderfully alive and irresistible *Things Carried Over* and Meg Tuite's brilliantly sharp *The World Gravitates Toward the Ditch* with its hammer blow of an opening line.

Second prize goes to Chetna Maroo and *Wealth of Nations* – a work so accomplished in its atmosphere and mystery that it is hard to believe it is Chetna's first published story. There is no doubt that it will be the first of many.

And our winner for 2017 is Dima Alzayat's extremely powerful and unforgettable *Ghusl*. It has moved and remained with all of us who have been lucky enough to read it and is a more-than-worthy champion in our 10th year.

And now that these prize decisions are out in the open, the judges deserve great credit for their discretion in keeping the results to themselves for 3 months, or 99 days to be precise!

One of the great joys of this competition is discovering the identity of the writers once all the judging decisions have been made. The stories are all read anonymously, with no knowledge of the authors' identities or locations. And once again we're so pleased to be publishing an international line up with writers based in Australia, Canada, USA, Ireland, The Netherlands, Germany and Malta as well as those in the UK published in the book.

We introduced an extra page of content in last year's anthology when we published the longlist and the 'notable contenders' who had nearly made it on to longlist. This is something we'll be doing every year. We consider being selected for the longlist to be a huge achievement. So congratulations to all those who feature on the lists at the back of the anthology.

One of the highlights of our year is the cover design project we run with final year Illustration students at the University of the West of England. The students submit designs for the anthology cover from which we select a winner. It's an almost impossible task. The students have no idea of the stories that will feature in the anthology and receive the broadest of briefs. The work they produce each year is astounding. And we really thank them for giving us this opportunity and big thanks, also, to Illustration course leaders Chris Hill and Jonathan Ward at UWE whose enthusiasm for and commitment to the project make it such a joy.

This year's wonderful cover was designed by Harry Sussams. We loved the broad, universal sweep of the design and its confident, eye catching appeal. It's the work of someone who's going to be doing this kind of thing for as long as he wants.

Big thanks are also due to Tangent Books who have been publishing our anthologies for the last four years and bringing them to a wider audience. Our developing association with them bodes well for the future.

And, most importantly, we offer our biggest thanks to all those writers who have had the courage to submit a story to us not only this year but over the past decade. We feel genuinely honoured that so many stories have been sent our way.

We hope you enjoy and relish these stories as much as we have and here's to another 10 years!

Joe Melia, BSSP Coordinator.

1st Prize
Dima Alzayat

Dima Alzayat is a Syrian-American writer. Her short stories have appeared in *Prairie Schooner*, *Bridport Prize Anthology*, and *Enizagam*. She was the recipient of a 2015 Bernice Slote Award. Her short story *In the Land of Kan'an* was included in artist Jenny Holzer's projection *For Aarhus* and is part of Holzer's 2017 exhibition at the Massachusetts Museum of Contemporary Art. Her articles have appeared in the *Los Angeles Times*, *Flaunt*, *The Skinny*, and *Variety*. She lives in Manchester, England, and is a PhD student and associate lecturer at Lancaster University.

Ghusl

Under the bright lights the skin had turned a whitish gray. A bandage wrapped around the face kept the mouth closed and flattened the black hair, made the chin thick and shapeless and pushed the cheeks towards shut lids. Rolled towels beneath the head and neck lifted the shoulders slightly from the metal bed, and under the white sheet the big toes were strung together with twine.

I will do it myself, she had said. *Haraam, haraam,* the men had replied and she had laughed inches from their faces. *And what is this? Is this not also sin?* They had waited with her for the coroner's van, had unlocked the room and shown her where the materials were kept. After they lifted and placed him on the table the eldest among them turned to her once more. *Sister, let us prepare him.* The rest shifted their eyes as she moved closer to the table, uncovered his face and asked them to leave.

Towels and sheets, white and folded, were stacked on the counter next to a plastic bucket and washcloths. She washed her hands in the sink and let the hot water run until her fingers became red and raw, the rough soap granules burrowing beneath her nails. When she put the gloves on they were tight and pinched her damp skin and she pulled them off and set them on the counter. The hygiene mask stayed in its box and the incense stick stood unlit in its holder.

With a washcloth wrapped around her hand she lifted the half-filled bucket and turned towards the table where he lay. The skin to her looked coated in silver dust, like the ashes that remain after the burning of a great tree. *Up we go.* With her right hand at the nape of his neck she lifted his head and shoulders and with the left slowly and gently pressed down on his stomach, keeping cloth between fingers and skin. Several times she pressed and released, and without completely lifting the sheet wiped and cleaned between the legs in short, quick moves.

Hanna who is small

    fell

        in a well   *he got stung by wasps*

  poor Hanna

    poor Hanna

      how

          did

    you

     fall?

Again at the counter she washed her hands and cleaned the bucket. Even with her back to him she could still see his face. The thin closed lids and the green eyes beneath them, the muscle that strained against the skin and made it pliant to its shape. If she stood very still she could see him sit up on the steel table and swing his legs over its edge. He would look around and catch his image in the mirror on the wall. *How funny I look ya Zaynab.* She gripped the counter to steady herself as warm water filled the bucket.

Where are you?

When she turned around he was still on his back, the green eyes shut and the lips a pale violet. *Look at us playing hide and seek, even now.* She carried the bucket and a clean washcloth to the table and set them down, took her time wetting the cloth, dipping it into the bucket and squeezing it several times until there was nothing left to do but begin. She moved the sheet and looked at the hands once so small. *Give me your hand ya Hamoud.* Cleaning now between the fingers of hands bigger than hers, moving from the smallest to the thumb.

this is Mr. Tall
and useless

this is the
labneh licker

and this is
the ring wearer

This is uncle
Abu Hatem

this is the
nit killer.

She wet the washcloth again and touched it to the forehead and slowly worked it over the eyes, the moisture clinging to thick lashes, and down the nose, her hand hesitating above the faded scar that began at the bridge and zigzagged down to the right and disappeared. He was three when he had fallen and she was nine and she had been chasing him up and down the hallway when he slipped on the black and white tiles and his giggles turned to wails. She had picked him up and held him as blood gushed from the wound between his eyes. He had clung on to her so tightly, had pulled on the skin of her neck as he cried, would not release her even when their father came running into the room.

Her eyes moved to the top of the head, the gauze that covered, concealed. *We'll clean it*, the hospital nurse had said. She had wanted to say *No*, dizzied by the thought of more hands she did not know, touching and prodding and taking. Now, her eyes fixed on the cloth until she willed them to shift, to follow instead the washcloth she ran over each arm, right and then left, flattening the small hairs against the skin. Within seconds they began to dry and she watched them shrink back into curls. She looked at the hair on her own arms, not much lighter or finer, and a smile flashed across her face and disappeared. Neither one wanting to wait for the other, they used to stand side by side at the sink to make wudu before prayer, take turns running arms beneath the faucet, carrying with cupped hands water to wet their hair and clean their mouths and noses, their necks and ears.

She waited for her breath to steady before her hand again reached towards the bandage and this time worked around it, wiping the black hair that jutted out in thick locks. Hair that once was combed back and gelled, or let loose and framed the face, played against the skin. She held her hand still and inhaled, reached the cloth's corner below the bandage and cleaned behind one ear and then the next, circled their grooves and ridges. *Even now you tickle me ya Zaynab.* She could hear the low giggle that clambered in pitch and tumbled into a steady roll, the sounds coming closer together, the depth of the final laugh that allowed her to exhale. When she moved to the feet, she put the cloth down and with her wet hands washed one foot at a time, reached between the toes, and massaged each sole.

The men should do this, they had insisted while waiting for the van to arrive.

And who are they to me, these men? Or to him?

Still they persisted. *You will need more people, Ms. Zaynab. Three or four, at least, to lift and turn and wrap.*

I have lifted him before, she had hissed. *I will remember how to do it, Inshallah.*

The bucket again cleaned and re-filled, she dropped from her palm the ground lote leaves they had given her. She watched the green powder float on the water's surface. *Will you be dust now ya Hamoud?* She stood beside the table and looked at his face. When they were children he would sometimes lie still while they took turns playing surgeon and patient and whoever moved or laughed first when poked with plastic knives or tickled with cotton swabs would lose. *Let's wash you.*

Upper right side and then upper left, she knew, then bottom right and left. Head to toe. From his body the water trickled down into the table's grooved perimeter, ran down to the opening that drained into a second bucket placed there. She held her breath as she loosened the bandage and paused to watch the mouth. When she saw that the lips stayed closed, a sound left her own mouth, a sigh that escaped from the floor of her chest and burst the room's stillness. She would not lift the bandage completely, would not with her hands touch where she knew the bones would give, where tissues and nerves like sponges would sink beneath her fingers. From the cloth she squeezed enough water to wet what hair was visible, from her palm dribbled more over the back of the head. Down the neck and over the shoulder she worked the cloth, across the chest and down to the navel. When she tilted him on his left side so she could reach his back she was surprised at his weight, and felt her arm muscles strain to keep him from slipping.

The last time she had picked him up he was ten and reached her shoulders in height. Their father had not come home from work and her mother sat in the kitchen whispering into the telephone in between splintered sobs and breaths that dissolved in the cold air. She had found her brother on the living room carpet shaking. He had wet his pants and a silent panic had pinned him to the floor, would not let his body do anything but tremble like a final leaf on a winter tree. She hoisted him up, her arm around his waist, and asked him to walk. But his legs continued to quaver and she knew then he could not stand, and in one move lifted him and wrapped her arms around his legs. In the bathroom she undressed him and sat him in the bathtub, and only when she made the deep low sounds of a freight ship and splashed her hands like fish pirouetting out of the water did the shaking stop.

Keeping the sheet over his torso she reached beneath it, cloth wrapped around her fingers, and cleaned underneath and between the legs, down the right leg to the toes and then the left. Thoughts of unknown hands that might have touched where she now did, their intentions different and beyond the things she knew, she forced from her mind. A strangeness remained in their place. She knew she would have to repeat it all. Three times, five times, nine. *Until you smell like the seventh heaven, like Sidrat al-Muntaha itself.* But with each repetition, her hand grew less certain, what it felt unfamiliar, and she glanced several times at the face in reminder as she wiped.

When she filled the bucket one last time, the colorless camphor dissolved in the water and released a smell that reminded her of mothballs and eucalyptus, of rosemary and berries. She removed the sheet still covering him and left only the small cloth spread from navel to knees. In the fluorescent light his bared body looked long and broad, and she thought of once-smaller hands she had cupped in hers, narrower shoulders she had held. From head to feet she poured the water and inhaled the scent that rose as the water ran along the table's gutter and splashed inside the plastic bucket.

I saw a butterfly with my eyes

        flitting

    it was   *around*

     me

          I ran trying to catch it, but it   *escaped*

from my hands.

    Where is the butterfly?

      It flew

                    away.

She unfolded one of the large towels and began to dry him. Gently she lifted his head, dried his hair one thick lock at a time, felt the water soak through the cotton and onto her hands. The skin of her fingertips shriveled from so much water. *They might never dry again ya Hamoud.*

The day they returned her father, with clenched fists her mother had beaten her own chest, pulled handfuls of hair from her scalp until the neighbors came. Her brother screamed for doctors until a neighbor came running and pulled him away. She was old enough to know that no doctors were needed, that what now lay in the courtyard, covered in burns and cuts and skin that curled back to reveal shredded muscle and blood clotted and congealed was a body she no longer knew.

She stepped back and looked at the body before her now, clean and damp. She scanned for places she had missed, where she might again pour the water and run the cloth. At the sound of the door opening behind her she moved closer to the table before turning to see the same older man from before, the only one who had spoken to her. A younger man followed and between them they wheeled a table, smaller and without grooves. She stepped aside and stood silent as they positioned it next to the table where he lay, but when the younger one began to unfold the stacked shrouds, she drew closer, placed her hand on his and made it still. With eyes wide he pulled his hand away and stepped back, but when he opened his mouth to speak, the older man leaned towards him and whispered words that kept him quiet. *Wallah they don't know what to make of this ya Zaynab.* She could hear the amused tone, the smile in the voice.

Two large sheets she unwrapped and placed, one atop the other, on the empty table. The smaller sheet she carried to where he lay, and unfolded over his body as they watched. Her hands hesitated when the sheet reached his neck and she could not lift all of him at once, she knew. She drew back enough to allow the men to move to either side of her, her fists clenching at her sides when with gloved hands they reached for him. As they lifted him the neck gave way and the head tilted back and she pressed her feet to the concrete floor. After they lowered him onto the second table and the head again rested flat, the older man reached beneath the sheet and removed the cloth covering the thighs. The younger man gripped the sheet's corners and began to pull it higher. She moved towards him. Stood close enough to feel the youthful swell of his belly protrude and recede with each breath, to make out the nose hairs that shivered as he drew air. Again the older man intervened, held the younger by the elbow and led him towards the door.

With the soil still new on her father's grave, they had come for her brother. Men with masked faces and heavy boots who slapped her grandfather across the face and threatened to tear off her clothes as her mother watched. *And like a good boy you sat so quietly.* In the kitchen cupboard behind pots and jars and sacks of rice and flour. When they left they took her grandfather with them, and the blood drops from her mother's nose spread like petals on the tiles.

She stood now at the counter mixing the sandalwood paste in a small bowl. Over and over she inhaled the scent and tried to keep her hands steady. *You will smell like the earth, ya Hamoud, like a tree and its soil.* Back where he lay, his face still uncovered, with her fingers she dabbed the paste onto his forehead and nose and rubbed it in, but still the brown tinted his pale face. With his hand in hers she worked the paste into one palm and then the next, reached beneath the sheet and dabbed the knees, and then the feet. She wished it were her feet on the table, her legs, her body. Imagined his hands stained brown as he touched her forehead instead. But his face, as she imagined it, contorted in silent grief, pushed the thought from her mind.

The three of them had arrived in a new country seeking darkness, the quiet of unlit rooms and the absence of knocks. A place where names had no meaning. Together they searched for the missing pieces of their mother, the stories that had shed their words. Not knowing why, she felt relief when he grew taller and bigger than she was. When he was found in the early morning hours behind the shop where he worked, his skull opened and spilling blood that ran through the black hair and onto the asphalt, she had been the one to call for doctors.

I had a little bird.

I looked after him,

and when his feathers grew and he was big,
he started to peck my cheeks

Zik zik zik zik zeek

19

Gently now she bent the left arm so that the palm flattened against the chest, folded the right arm so that the right palm rested on the left. *And this is how we pray ya Hamoud.* When he was six she had taught him how to pray. Her parents laughed that he was too young, but she had spent years waiting for him to grow, to learn words and what they meant, so that she could show him things, teach him what she knew; the alphabet and how to ride a bike, the names of animals alive and extinct, the planets in the solar system and their moons. So when she stood beside him on the prayer rug and told him to move as she did, he did as he was told, touching hands to chest and then to knees, forehead touching the carpet and back up again. For years after he would only pray if she led.

She stood beneath the bright lights, her fingertips grazing the sheet's edge. Her eyes traced the arc of his brows, the hairs that strayed from their place. She imagined what they looked like when he smiled, the way they drew together, and noticed for the first time the thin lines near his eyes. *Whose eyes will see us now?* Her mother, she knew, would never speak again. Her own words as she pulled the sheet above the mouth and then higher still were like boats with neither sails nor oars.

After the sheets were wrapped around him, the center looped with ropes, the ends fastened, she stood with empty hands. *Make me like a sandwich ya Zaynab.* She would have him lie on the bed sheet and roll him from one end to the other, and through the layers she could hear his giggles. If her mother or father was walking by, they laughed with them. *Make sure he can breathe ya Zaynab.*

2nd Prize
Chetna Maroo

Chetna Maroo was born in Nairobi, Kenya. She grew up in England and currently lives in London, where she is working on a collection of short stories.

Wealth of Nations

It was her father who had taken her to Mr Dodhia's shop, the first time. It was long ago, before she had changed her name, before she had buried herself west of the city where she could not be found. She had been eleven, maybe twelve.

They had driven up in her father's new black car with its new leather seats. The whole day had smelled of leather. Her father had told her she would have to sit quietly in the car while he talked to Mr Dodhia. He was there to offer Mr Dodhia a contract. After he told her that, he had looked at her in his mild, expectant way.

'What are the terms of the contract?' she had asked quietly. And even though she wasn't looking, she knew her father was nodding his approval.

'We will take twenty percent of his earnings.'

'*Twenty*…' She stopped. She fixed her attention on a fly that had landed on her side of the windscreen. 'What will he…what will the counterparty get?'

Before she could move away, her father had reached over and was awkwardly patting her shoulder. 'Good girl,' he said. She smelled peppermint on his breath. 'You see, the counterparty has had some trouble. He needs protection. So we will protect him.' It was a plain fly; blue, she thought, or green, and hump-backed. She looked away but her father took her chin lightly between his thumb and forefinger, brought her back round. 'For someone like him, it's a good offer. Right?'

'Yes,' she said. The fly, taking off, seemed to shimmer.

'You'd best not spend the whole time reading that nonsense,' her father said gently, hauling himself out of the car. She looked at the book in her hands, then returned her gaze to the fly on the windscreen as she reached down to her school bag and slipped the book inside.

Her father was in Mr Dodhia's shop for a long time, and when he came out, his face was pink and ugly.

Mr Dodhia had refused his offer.

She saw her father spit casually on the '*Toys and Buggies*' sign outside the shop while Mr Dodhia watched from the doorway. Mr Dodhia stood like a giant, his eyes dark beneath his colossal brow. Her father took a white brick from a pile of rubble near the road. The two men faced each other across the pavement.

She remembered how she had concentrated on Mr Dodhia's massive hands that hung at his sides, how she had pressed her face against the car window to see how fast those hands would move if her father launched the brick. But her father had no intention of doing so. He was a gentle man; he did only what he had to do. He had often told her that. He walked unhurriedly round the back of the car to climb into the driver's seat and, once inside, he handed her the brick. It was lighter than she had imagined. She held it in both hands and when her father started the car engine, she felt Mr Dodhia's gaze shift; his eyes met hers through the car window. She stared at his great sad dark face. It had begun to rain. That face is like granite, she thought; the rain will sink into it. She wondered how it would feel to touch that face.

Mr Dodhia was the first to look away. She saw at once what it was that had caught his attention: something fluttered slowly over the back of his hand. She could see the shimmer of blue. He kept on looking at it while the car began to pull away and in those few seconds, while they both gazed at that shimmering blue fly, she knew for the first time that she wasn't quite alone.

On the morning of her eighteenth birthday, Rosalind Parker thought about her father, as she always did. And as she always did, she resolutely drove him from her mind. She dressed, put on her good coat and made her way into the city. She pushed ahead of her a buggy whose frame was scratched and warped and whose brakes no longer functioned because she had deliberately broken them the night before. She was going to buy a new buggy: her third. Rosalind had worked away at her old buggy with a spanner and the heel of her shoe, trying not to think about how Mr Dodhia would look at her when she turned up at his shop yet again.

She went via the backstreets, stopping only once, at the library where she worked during the week. She left the buggy and went inside. When she came out she had a bag of books, which she was placing carefully on the seat when a young man hurrying past – a boy, really, maybe no older than sixteen – bumped her shoulder and slammed his briefcase against the side of the buggy. She began to object. She wanted to say something devastating, something to shame him, but she saw the shabbiness of his coat, the way his trouser legs hung about his calves and she imagined that he was on his way to some basement office where he would spend his days checking contracts because it was what he had been bred to do, and she said nothing. She looked at the blue, cloudless sky. She rearranged the bag on the seat of her buggy, pushed back her hair, and walked on.

As soon as she turned onto Bell Street, Rosalind saw that Mr Dodhia's windows had been smashed in again.

Someone – it could only have been Mr Dodhia himself – had gathered the stones and bricks that had been hurled at the shop, and piled them against the shop's front wall. Rosalind glanced down the street. It was empty. She levered her buggy over the curb and keeping one hand on the frame, she bent down. She chose a white stone that was rough and flat. She slipped it into her coat pocket and looked up.

It was still there: cardinal red, gold-lined, majestic.

Mustang, it was called.

It was all that was left of Mr Dodhia's window display. The brochure described the Mustang as a travel system, combining buggy and car seat, but Rosalind knew it was much more than that: she had watched Mr Dodhia kneeling heavily beside the Mustang to polish its chrome, his massive, scarred hands brisk and precise, his ragged lip close to the metal so that its surface was misted by his breath. Rosalind thought about Mr Dodhia's hands moving over the frame and she almost reached up to touch it. Her fingers trembled. The rapturous feeling that came over her faded only when she pushed open the door of Mr Dodhia's shop and heard the familiar ding-ding that announced her entrance.

Mrs Dodhia stood behind the counter.

Rosalind forced her buggy through the doorway, catching her purse on the door handle. Mrs Dodhia pulled her shawl tight over her shoulders and smiled; amiable, uncomprehending.

'My husband comes,' Mrs Dodhia said, a softly defensive hand on the counter. Her hand, Rosalind thought, was too slight for the gold bangle that adorned it. Mr Dodhia would have placed the bangle there, pushing it over the knuckle, onto the wrist. The hand was so slender that Mr Dodhia would have met no resistance. Rosalind shoved her own hands into her coat pockets. She scanned the shop. It was small and over-crowded with goods, most of the buggies and toys from the window display now crammed onto the shop floor. Against one wall leaned the plywood boards that, before the end of the day, Mr Dodhia would fix where the windows had been. Rosalind took in the chaos and wondered if Mr Dodhia was upstairs at his desk. Or out in the city, pressing into the crowds, his great coat over his shoulders.

My husband comes, Mrs Dodhia had said, and that was about all she ever said.

My husband comes. There was something at once helpless and possessive in her repetition of the phrase.

Rosalind closed her fist around the stone inside her pocket and attempted a friendly smile. Mrs Dodhia smiled back; then, quietly, she cleared her throat and switched on the fluorescent ceiling lights. Mrs Dodhia's dull pink shawl caught this new light brilliantly. It seemed to glow a pretty rose-gold, and it made her skin glow too. Some men would have considered Mrs Dodhia a beauty in this light.

Rosalind looked away. She swept her fingers along one shoulder as though she were removing a speck of dirt. At the same time, she checked her reflection in the mirrored door behind Mrs Dodhia. Her own hands were too big, masculine, like her shoulders, and she knew without looking that her complexion was pale and not pretty at all. She let her hand fall and, slowly, she turned her chin. Her hair fell over her shoulders then, in large, luminous curls. Her hair, she knew, was magnificent. And when she angled her face a certain way, her round eyes gave her a sweet, holy look. She smiled discreetly at her reflection, just as one of the Dodhia children – a girl – stuck her head round the mirrored door. The girl's eyes met Rosalind's, then drifted to Rosalind's hair.

Mrs Dodhia must have indicated to her daughter that she was welcome because the girl slipped forward until she was somehow nestled in the folds of Mrs Dodhia's skirt. The girl's eyes were alert and small. She peered up at her mother as if to check she was coping and, satisfied, she returned her gaze to Rosalind's hair.

The girl's attention made Rosalind feel strangely drowsy. She rubbed slowly, absent-mindedly, at a knot at the base of her neck. She wondered what the world looked like for this clever, melancholy child. Was she afraid? Did she think, with an open, fearful heart, about this country to which her father had brought her? Did she think it was defined by the thugs who called out in the street that she should go home or by the sound of smashing glass or by her mother's silence? Did she think about it at all?

Rosalind moved quickly to the counter.

'I'm so sorry,' she said. 'About the windows.'

Mrs Dodhia smiled. 'My husband comes,' she said.

The door dinged and Mr Dodhia strode into his shop.

He removed his coat and handed it to Mrs Dodhia and for a moment the heavy expression on his face seemed to ease. He is glad to be in his shop, Rosalind thought. And then she thought that it must have begun to rain because Mr Dodhia's disheveled hair glistened and the smell of it – the smell of the rain – filled the place.

'Miss Rosalind,' he said, his voice harsh as he placed his palm on the head of his daughter, who had skipped forward and who now laughed, ducked and skipped back behind the counter.

'Mr Dodhia,' Rosalind replied, and there she stopped, blushing and confused. The last time she had spoken his name out loud, they had been alone in the shop. Mr Dodhia had been reaching up to the display window and she didn't know what had come over her but she had moved close to him, so close she could smell the soap on his shirt. She had stood in his shadow imagining that he felt everything that she felt. She had said his name, and he had swept his glance over her. A wicked light shines in his eyes, she had thought, a light that's old and mysterious and… no, not wicked, exactly. She had stared at him, trying to work out what it was. And he had swallowed and she had watched his Adam's apple rise and fall and he had turned away. And there was a part of her that was glad.

'It's my buggy,' Rosalind said, at last. 'The brakes.'

Mr Dodhia swung round abruptly and approached the buggy, which she had parked near the door. Rosalind wanted to stop him but he was already leaning down, inspecting the chassis, moving it about, taking care not to disturb the bag on the seat. Beneath his shirt, the muscles in his shoulders rose.

'I can fix it,' he said, straightening, but his low, abrasive voice made it seem as though he had announced that he would break it.

'Mr Dodhia,' Rosalind said, quickly, 'I want a new one. *That* one,' and she pointed behind him, at the Mustang.

The shop was quiet.

Mr Dodhia said, 'This is a good buggy.' He placed a hand on the frame of Rosalind's buggy.

'The other one has pneumatic tyres,' Rosalind said.

'You take your buggy into the jungle?' Mr Dodhia asked, slowly, deliberately.

'I don't,' she answered, and her face and neck became warm and then hot because she liked him so much. She looked into his eyes. She took a deep breath.

'The Mustang,' she said, 'is everything I ever wanted.'

Mr Dodhia stared at her.

'No,' he said. 'It is not.'

Mrs Dodhia began to move about, as though she had at that second decided to tidy the counter. Rosalind looked desperately in Mrs Dodhia's direction and, feeling the plea, Mrs Dodhia glanced up briefly and smiled her amiable smile.

When Mr Dodhia spoke again, it seemed to be with great effort. 'Miss Rosalind,' he said, 'all of my buggies are good. But if you keep on buying new ones, the manufacturers will take advantage. They'll build new buggies with impossible new features but they will be cheaply made and quick to fail. Only the manufacturers will profit.'

Rosalind didn't know how to answer. Mr Dodhia knew she had no child and no need of a buggy; he knew – he must know – why she came into his shop, why she bought his goods; and he stood there discussing who would profit.

She wanted to tell him that he was a good man.

Mr Dodhia waited.

She glanced behind him, at the Mustang, whose gold edging glinted under his lights.

'But isn't that progress?' she said, quickly. 'The manufacturers will reinvest their profits, and then won't we all be better off?'

Mr Dodhia seemed to sway. His lip stretched outward. His eyes shone.

'You've been reading *The Wealth of Nations*?' he asked.

His voice was so harsh and close that it was like a vibration in her chest. Rosalind wondered if he had caught in his jaws the bricks that had been thrown into his shop, if he had broken them down and held the wreckage inside his mouth in order to speak to her like that.

'Mr Dodhia,' she said, 'I admire you, I admire your principles, but you cannot feed your children on good principles.'

'No,' he replied, the gleam still in his eyes. 'I cannot.'

Mr Dodhia had told her he would deliver the Mustang.

At six-thirty, Rosalind stood before her mirror, brushing her hair. Already its whole length seemed to shine with its own light. She kept on brushing. She wondered what the little Dodhia girl would think if she saw it now. She let the brush drop to the floor, reached behind her for a lipstick. She moved closer to the mirror and quickly she touched her lips with the rose colour.

In half an hour he would be there, in her home. She put the kettle on and wiped the narrow worktop. She took down a shoebox from above the fridge, opened the lid and carefully removed layers of tissue. She lifted out a silver tray. It was plain and beautiful. She placed it on the worktop. Slowly, she unwrapped four round almond biscuits and arranged them in a pyramid on one half of the tray. On the other half, she placed two little cakes layered with raspberry jam. She sprinkled sugar on top. She took her time about it. When she had finished, she stepped back, wiping her hands on her skirt.

She checked the clock and went through the loosely hung curtain that divided the room in two. She began to look at the books that lay in piles on the floor around her mattress. Mr Dodhia had asked her about *The Wealth of Nations*. She had nothing like that. Something different then, she thought, something important. She glanced out of the little window that looked directly onto the window of her neighbour's empty spare room. She wondered if she had time to lie down.

As soon as she heard the clang of the gate in front of her block, Rosalind stopped in the middle of the room, and then she was crossing to the worktop to switch the kettle on again and after that she was simply standing there, waiting for the buzzer to sound.

'Mr Dodhia,' she blurted into the intercom.

By the time Mr Dodhia finally knocked on her door, having climbed the three flights of stairs with the boxed up Mustang in his arms, Rosalind was shaking.

'Just here, I think, next to the window, it's good of you to bring it.'

'A pleasure,' he said.

She inhaled the smell of rain. She watched his face; he looked less sullen, more yielding. It was the light. She touched her hair.

'You'll take tea,' she said. 'Or something else?'

Mr Dodhia looked at her, then glanced about the room, taking in the emptiness of it. Rosalind wished she had bought flowers, lots of them.

'Tea, then,' he said.

Rosalind nodded. She managed to tell him to sit, but he seemed to prefer to stand. He picked up the book she had placed on the arm of the sofa, he held it in both hands. He turned it over. Rosalind moved about the kitchen.

'*War and Peace*,' he said. 'What do you think of it?'

'Oh.' She glanced over her shoulder. 'It is *life itself*.'

When she saw that he had finally sat down and was reading the back cover on which the words she had just spoken were printed in pale gold letters, she stopped. He looked up. He looked into her eyes. He smiled, but she could see his mind was elsewhere.

Stiffly, she set on the table in front of him the tea cups, the silver tray with the biscuits and raspberry cakes, two small plates, two forks, two glasses of water. She sat down on the sofa, beside him. Mr Dodhia was still wearing his coat. His coat was damp against her bare arm; damp and cold. She clasped her hands together, pressed them despairingly into her lap. She stared at the two cakes she had dusted with sugar. She wanted to shout at him to look at her. She wanted to shout at him to take off his coat.

'Does Mrs Dodhia like to read?' she asked.

'Nirmala? No.'

There was silence.

And then he added, 'She likes music. And she likes to dance, a little.'

To dance. That was news. Rosalind couldn't imagine Mr Dodhia's wife dancing. She couldn't imagine *Nirmala* dancing. It was the first time she had heard Mrs Dodhia's name; she wished that Mr Dodhia hadn't mentioned it.

She likes music. And she likes to dance, a little. Rosalind felt a suffocating impulse to cause Mrs Dodhia harm. It was the qualification that did it: 'a little'. Those two words were loaded with something intimate and intensely physical between Mr and Mrs Dodhia: Mr Dodhia wishing quietly, perhaps, that Mrs Dodhia might like to dance a little more so that he could watch her from a corner of the room, eyes narrowed to see her better; or Mrs Dodhia drifting in his arms as he urged, rough and close and quiet so that only she could hear, 'One more, Nirmala.'

But none of that mattered, Rosalind told herself, it couldn't matter. Mrs Dodhia did not read or have opinions and she barely spoke, and Mr Dodhia was a thinker. Hadn't he smiled when he asked her if she had been reading *The Wealth of Nations?* Wasn't there something particular in that smile, something more significant than a little dancing?

'What do you think Mrs Dodhia would say about Tolstoy?' Rosalind asked, taking a biscuit from the top of the pyramid.

Mr Dodhia turned his head and looked at Rosalind and it gave her a jolt. It was that same look. Old and mysterious and – this time Rosalind understood what else it was in Mr Dodhia's eyes that were suddenly so bright. It was pity. Mr Dodhia, whose windows were smashed in, felt sorry for her.

Mr Dodhia returned his gaze to the table.

'My wife is a quiet woman,' he said.

Rosalind put down her cup, slowly, so that it wouldn't clatter.

In those few words was everything: Mr Dodhia's wife; his children; his shop; his life, in the city. There was nothing else. Rosalind understood, then, that Mr Dodhia loved Mrs Dodhia, deeply. His life with her was not a burden, it was everything he wanted and the only thing he could imagine.

It was the only thing he could imagine. That thought seemed to quieten something in Rosalind; she noticed its effect curiously, unemotionally, as though she was observing someone she didn't know lying down in the street.

Without thinking, she stood up. On the windowsill was the white stone she had picked up outside Mr Dodhia's shop. She must have taken it from her pocket when she had returned home. She held it on her palm for a minute. She felt calm.

Mr Dodhia considered the stone and then raised his eyes to hers as if to say: Is this what I've come here to discuss? The sun slanting through the window lit his face; and though his skin was grey and broken, his lip was less ragged than she had thought it, his eyes less sunken beneath his brow. She wanted to touch his face. She wanted to start talking to him about the time she and her father had paid him a visit. She knew there was something specific she should say.

'I never read it,' she said, suddenly.

Mr Dodhia put his cup next to hers on the table and said nothing.

'The book,' she explained. '*War and Peace.*' And she found that once she had begun speaking, she couldn't stop. 'I mean… years ago, but I don't remember. Or… something about a cabin in the woods, a tray – biscuits with rye and buttermilk, brandy – a countess throwing off her shawl to dance. I remember that.'

His eyes met hers.

'I remember that,' she said, again.

Later, when Mr Dodhia had gone, Rosalind sank back down in front of the empty cups and untouched glasses of water. She felt a vague urge to tip one of the glasses, so that the water would fall slowly over her hand, onto the bare wood and below, through the cracks in the floor. She touched the glass. She got up. She went over to the white box containing the Mustang. Probably, it was enclosed in bubble wrap inside the box. Probably, Mrs Dodhia had held down the edges while Mr Dodhia maneuvered himself around her, fixing the tape, taking care not to catch his wife's fingers. She put her hand on the box, but did not move to open it. She stood like that for a long time, looking out of the window. It was a fine evening. The earlier rain had wet the ground and now it shone like gold in the glow of the sun that was sinking but had not yet sunk below the horizon and the flies that rose from the ground shimmered with their familiar blue light. Rosalind smiled. She lifted her fingers from the Mustang and put her hand against the glass. In Mr Dodhia's room above the shop and the broken windows there would be music, she thought, and a little dancing.

3rd Prize
Bunmi Ogunsiji

Bunmi Ogunsiji received an MA in Screenwriting from University of the Arts London and is a Nigerian-British South London-based writer, mother of a bright, sardonic teenager, blogger (bunmiogunsiji.com), resurrected Performance Poet and writer. Her work has been longlisted and shortlisted in a number of writing competitions including *Mslexia* Flash Fiction Competition and Bath Flash Fiction Award. A lover of yoga, avocado and most things green she cites amongst her finest achievements: turning 50 with a smile and honouring her feet with a pair of comfortable walking shoes.

Things Carried Over

"It's 1.8 miles. That's 2.9 kilometres in length." Trump's Muslim ban, Brexit, the refugee crisis, environmental pollution, North Korean nuclear missile tests, global warfare, homelessness, and all Ravi, the library's resident idiot savant aka facilities officer wants to talk about is Streatham High Road. Ravi's in his fifties, a Wikipedia junkie with a fuzz of jet black and grey curls, an abnormally large head and an aberrant penchant for hologram socks which he usually wears under Birkenstock sandals. He's followed me into the Tate room, despite my best efforts to lose him en route, and is now standing next to Sir Henry Tate's bust, staring gormlessly through the window, his hands tucked deep into the pockets of a Senegalese Boubou, donned, I assume in honour of Black History month. He dresses for the occasion every year. Last year it was a Kente tunic and the year before that, traditional Nigerian attire: the Agbada. He's wearing something on his head with this year's costume: a Fila cap. Ravi doesn't mind mixing his cultural paraphernalia: Nigerian Fila cap, Senegalese Boubou, Christmas hologram socks.

"Begins north at Streatham Hill railway station being an end-on junction with Streatham Hill and continues south to Norbury where the A23 becomes London Road." For the past few months Ravi's made it his mission to follow me around the library like a benevolent stalker. Can't help feeling he's waiting for something, for me to say or do something. *Drop* something.

I shuffle the flyers on a nearby display table and pretend to be conscientious but the truth is, I'm not here, just going through the motions while I try to figure out how to end things with Pasha. Pasha. Six years together. My best friend. My partner. Haven't touched her in six months. We haven't spoken, really spoken in that time. Turns out, her miscarriage, third in a row, is a conversation killer. I'm the problem, she says, with the *'closed-encounters-hold it-down'* thing I've got going on. "It's 2016, a new age," she said through her tears as I dismantled the Mothercare Stretton cot-bed in the baby's room. "Men cry. Black men cry."

Ravi crouches down and starts fumbling with something behind the radiator. He does this often. Fumbles. Fumbles with light fittings, plugs, blinds, staffroom appliances, but never fixes anything or more to the point, never arranges for anything to be fixed. The following scenario happens on a regular basis, it plays on a loop: I go into facilities to ask about long overdue repairs to a faulty toilet or a murmuring radiator still murmuring after five weeks or the ominous flickering of LED lights, only to be dragged by my teeth into a monologue starting with something obscure like the origins of postcodes and ending with the cultural importance of 'Stormzy'. And always, I'm told by Ravi he's on the case regarding the repairs. He never is.

"Streatham High Street. Some say it's a strong contender for the longest continuous high street in Europe, which is complete nonsense given that Piotrkowska in Poland is substantially longer at 4.9km."

Ravi is an imbecile. I catch him sometimes just smiling at his socks. Who does that?

"You OK Or *Ray*?"

I hate the way he splits my name into two words rather than two syllables as in Or Ray with emphasis on the *Ray*. My first day working at the library I arrived early to find Ravi looking anything but secure on the highest rung of a metal ladder, fumbling with something inside the security box by the front entrance. His fascination with my name began then.

"Or *Ray*. Like the young lad who won Strictly this year? You watch that? He did a mean Argentine tango. Really good. You look a little like him actually. You're not him, are you?" His face broke into a sunny grin, perfect baby teeth on display.

"It's short for something right?"

"Oreoluwa."

"Where's it from?"

"Nigeria."

"It's got a meaning right?"

"Gift from God."

"I like that. Like that a lot. My name's Ravi." He raised his eyebrows, lowered them and raised them again. My cue to express a similar interest in the origins of his name but before I got the hint he offered the meaning.

"Sun."

Looking at him in his reindeer socks, his baggy denim dungarees, I knew then that I had encountered a universe unto itself: Planet Ravi.

I turn around and having exhausted his 'fumbling' activity, he's just standing there watching me intently, a quizzical look on his face like I'm an episode of 'Question Time' which he told me, with the plastic handle of a screwdriver hanging from his mouth while he was fumbling with something behind the photocopier, was his favourite programme.

"I'm not a movie Ravi."

"Sorry, you just seem a little out of sorts." He looks genuinely concerned.

I skulk over to the self-service kiosk where a Somalian mother is struggling to scan her kid's items under the machine's infra-red light. Winston, eighty-seven years old, only thirteen years from the great centenary he keeps telling everyone, passing wind in the paperback section, gives me his customary nod. Jocelyn oblivious to everything but the space in front of her, rocks back and forth in the purple chair by the returned items shelf, her ridiculously tight surgical stockings, doing the opposite of what they're intended for and compromising the circulation in her legs. Margaret over by the photocopier in her usual seat peers over the top of her Anne Perry novel every now and then like she's reading a top-secret document. Regulars. Some things never change, not even when the planet explodes.

I was neutral. About the baby. Shut-down. A self-protective device. Like I was bracing myself for impact. I heard her crying and knew before I opened the bathroom door, she'd be there, dazed and confused, sitting on the side of the bath, her night-shirt with the cute sheep on the front dotted with blood. And I was ready.

Margaret tuts disapprovingly as a toddler erupts out of the children's area brandishing a copy of 'The Tiger Who Came to Tea.' He careers into my legs, looks up at the giant I am and flashes me this smile. Could disarm Isis, that smile. I feel the cord around my gut tighten. I help the mother with her books.

"The machine has to read the bar code." I can hear my own irritation and straight away I feel guilty in case she thinks I'm being like that because she's Somalian. I scan the top two hardbacks for her and hear her say something in an angry whisper to a boy, must be ten, in a nearby chair, his head engrossed in Irvine Welsh's 'Trainspotting'. The boy snatches the picture book from the toddler then picks him up. The toddler gives me a wave he's probably just learned how to do, then chuckles and I feel the cord tighten a little more. The older boy hands his mother the 'Trainspotting' novel to scan. I try to tell the mother the book's probably not the best, most appropriate reading for a child his age but English is not her first language and she doesn't understand. I stop caring. I tell her she'll need to take it out on her card. The boy translates. She takes out her adult card to scan the book, the boy stands over his mum's shoulder, eyes me like a traitor and when they're leaving, gives me the finger.

I step out onto Pinfold Street for a cigarette break and rehearse what I'm going to say to Pasha. I tap out a text. *I love you but this isn't working.* I feel soulless. Who leaves his girlfriend after something like that? Suddenly, Ravi's there. He scurries over to the roadside and scrapes the bottom of his sandal against the kerb.

"Chewing gum on the floor in the children's room."

He takes out his tobacco and papers and rolls himself a cigarette.

"I don't have one you know." He moves in a little too close, leaning on the wall next to me like me and him are tight.

"A phone, I mean."

Ravi makes this weird sucking noise as he pulls on his cigarette. It's distracting.

"Best to look someone in the eye when you're talking to them. I mean if you need to call the gas man or it's something work related that's different. But nowadays people are so glued to the little screen they don't really have a clue what's going on around them. Technology is a virtual illusion. Flesh and bone connection, that's what it's all about Or *Ray*. Flesh and bone." After I manage to stamp dead the thought that Ravi could possibly be hitting on me it goes quiet inside, quiet as in ghost town quiet, and it hits me, the memory. And it stings. Like the hot chilli Pasha forgot to wash off her fingers before we slept together for the first time. She was sympathetic at first but cracked up when I hollered. Yeah, hollered like a girl. After several hours with my penis shoved in a bag of frozen peas I knew I loved her. We talked then talked some more and the morning came, snuck in while she was changing my world.

"Streatham's lost its heart you know. I mean look at the library. £1.4 million spent on a face lift and all these self-service machines. People don't talk to each other anymore."

I call Pasha, it rings and goes to voicemail.

In the outside garden area, away from Ravi's inane rambling I try Pasha again. Can't kick this need to speak to her. Her phone rings then goes to voicemail. Again. Suddenly it has me gasping for oxygen, the prospect of losing her. So, I try her again. Voicemail. I go back inside and Ravi's by the Black History month display table like he's guarding it or something. I'm lost for words, just when I think he can't get more fucking stupid he hits the zenith of dumb. He picks up Toni Morrison's 'Beloved', looks at me, says nothing, just holds it close to his chest and nods his head like he's mulling over something profound, someone, somewhere, once said to him at some point in time.

"You read this?" Ravi thinks I've read all the books on the table "Poignant, really poignant." He looks sad, the way he did when I came back to work after my leave. Bad fortune has a stench. Olga, couldn't stop apologizing, commiserating, then apologizing. Haran, gave me a wide berth, his wife was expecting, could be contagious. Melanie, couldn't speak to me for weeks, kept biting her bottom lip 'til it was raw, her head bowed down like she didn't want to see it: the hole. No one wanted to see it, or get close, except Ravi.

"She'd rather kill her own baby than see her daughter sold into slavery. Based on a true story you know. Margaret Garner, her name was." Despite myself I'm just a little impressed with his knowledge though too comforted by my familiar resentment of him to let on. It comes through then. A text. From Pasha. *Can't do this anymore Ore. Need to end this.* I read the text again and again thinking maybe if I look at it enough times it'll say something different. In the background, Ravi's twittering on about Ralph Ellison, his words rolling into one long sentence of nothing. I call Pasha again. Ravi raises his eyebrows and gestures to my phone.

"You don't want Olga having a go at you. She can be a dragon, that one." Voicemail. I can't breathe.

Ravi's entertaining himself with some joke and my head implodes.

"You can't make life better with fucking Christmas socks Ravi and no one, I mean *no one* Ravi gives a shit about your thoughts on the Invisible Man or the length of Streatham High Road!" I screech at Ravi in a high-pitched voice that doesn't belong to me, and his face eclipses over. Jocelyn stops rocking and stares at me like I'm the one with the mental health issue, Margaret slams shut the Anne Perry novel she's reading, like my meltdown is just annoying and Jim responds to my histrionics with a guttural fart. The library's suddenly a graveyard, and Ravi and I, we're in this thing together, whatever it is.

"Alright Or *Ray*, alright."

Then it happens, I see Ravi with his jet black, grey streaked hair and his Christmas socks and Senegalese Boubou and it reverberates in me, his tone, his calm, forgiving tone. It's like a feather and down pillow I can lay my sorrow on, and I lose it. I mean right there in the library in front of everyone, I start crying. I mean 'EastEnders' crying, eyes red raw can't breathe or stand up straight crying.

"You're in a bad way, aren't you" Just like Ravi to state the obvious. He puts his arm around my shoulder and leads me to his office.

"You're going to be alright. You know that don't you?" Ravi says, like he's some sage and he switches on the kettle. The threat of intimacy between us brings me back to myself and I have to normalise the moment with a little off-centre pragmatism.

"You know why I don't like books Ravi?"

He looks worried.

"They fill me with questions I don't really have room for in my life."

"But you're a librarian." Ravi says.

"Just because you work in a sewage plant doesn't mean you like faeces."

"You've got a point there Or *Ray*."

We don't say anything for a long time. Ravi looks at me and I have no control over the wave rising, hauling me up out of my comfort zone and crashing over me, so I'm balling again, like a girl. I cry for the baby. The two before. I cry for Pasha and me. Even for Ravi, standing there in his Boubou, watching over me.

"You go on Or *Ray*. Get it all out."

He pours the hot water into two mugs and spoons out the coffee.

"Nothing like caffeine to recalibrate a person."

He hands me the mug, but my arms are folded and I'm hugging myself trying to keep myself from disintegrating. Ravi puts the mug on the desk next to a picture of a black woman with a dazzling smile, in a regal Gelee and Buba, and a boy, on her lap, maybe seven, eight. Hadn't noticed that before on previous visits to Ravi's cave.

"Trouble at home?"

I nod my head yes.

"Figured as much. Obviously, I don't know your story. Why would I? No one's said anything to me but I have a sense Or *Ray*, a sixth sense when it comes to these things."

I don't have a clue what Ravi's talking about and want to tell him to shut up but the snot and tears are making it difficult for me to formulate expletives.

"You know, things carried. Even when people don't say."

The graveyard, the dead quiet again.

"Can I ask a question Or *Ray*?"

I nod my head yes.

"Can you fix it?"

"What?"

I find my voice through the phlegm and sorrow.

"Whatever's broken?"

I shrug my shoulders. Truth is, I don't know.

"My wife and I always found a way. When things were tough, we'd talk it through and then we'd find something to laugh about."

I gaze down at his thick, clumsy looking fingers and there it is, his wedding ring. I feel guilty in the moment for wondering why the hell anyone would do that to herself.

"Some things you can't laugh about Ravi."

I can't believe I'm talking to him. Ravi, the fountain of useless information, a pitifully abysmal dress sense and that idiotic smile. He didn't even have the good sense to be miserable or offended, angry even, when I slated him.

"Our first date we took the 159 all the way from one end of Streatham High Street to the other. Just for the fun of it. Never stopped talking. And we laughed. That was our marriage."

Ravi smiles at the woman in the picture.

"She loved Christmas. When she got sick she started buying me these Christmas socks, from Woolworth's, you know, when it was still around. She bought a whole bag full. *'To last you the year'* she said *'Something to make it feel like Christmas when I'm not here.'*"

He slurps his coffee then.

"Some things you can't fix Or *Ray*. But some things you can. If you can fix it and there's love there, then fix it."

Ravi pats me on the shoulder and walks out. For a minute, I don't know where I am. I don't know *who* I am. Who Ravi is. *Ravi.* I try Pasha again. This time she answers. Don't know why or how but I tell her a joke, take a chance, and I hear it, soft at first, then louder, her laugh. Like when I had my chilli crisis.

When I come out of Ravi's office, he's standing by the library entrance, a guardian of the gate, smiling at his socks.

3rd Prize
Meg Tuite

Meg Tuite is author of a novel-in-stories, *Domestic Apparition*, a short story collection, *Bound by Blue*, and won the Twin Antlers Collaborative Poetry Prize for her poetry collection, *Bare Bulbs Swinging*, as well as four chapbooks of short fiction, flash, and poetic prose. She teaches at Santa Fe Community College, is a senior editor at *Connotation Press* and *(b)OINK lit zine*, and editor of eight anthologies. Her work has been published in numerous literary magazines, over fifteen anthologies, and nominated nine times for the Pushcart Prize, five-time *Glimmer Train* finalist, and Gertrude Stein Award finalist. She blogs at: http://megtuite.com

The World Gravitates Toward the Ditch

After a lava lamp exploded through Dad's skull we found out that he was very much a family man. He traveled the tentacled vagrancy of a globe only a logical liar could have navigated. Three wives appeared at his funeral with slumped offspring that he'd pocketed in Omaha, North Platte, and Wahoo. And that was only from one state. That explained some of his archeological digs. He lived with us on and off for years. Mom and Dad had separate bedrooms.

"Your mother and I have a deep commitment to individuality," Dad said.

"Your father can't get it up and I have never been competitive," Mom said.

I was his last and only child born in New Mexico. There was vast interest and hunger for 'black light bulbs' in the '70's and Dad made his cash as a supplier, although Mom told me later, 'you'd have to sell a hellava lot of bulbs to bring home the backpacks full of cash weighing down that crappy Pinto of his'.

Dad's trips to the Himalayas, which now appeared to be Nebraska and peyote, had taken him on a journey where he told me he squatted and strained off the furthest hatch of land in hopes that his non-constipated avalanche would someday be petrified. The vault of his resounding being would dilate and spread through the landscape, like his offspring, and someone wading through the sacred river below in the future would hold it in his hands and penetrate his deepest thoughts. "It's a rock in the shape of a heart," he said. "What comes out of us is art, no matter the form."

"Close your eyes. Tell me what I'm thinking," he would say.

"Ice cream." He had cash and Mom's dessert was vodka.

His nose was central to his face, fiercely red and push-pinned with small dark planets that reminded me of the night sky in reverse.

"It's about your mom," he said. "Try again."

No. It was about frozen enchiladas and tamales for dinner that crunched between my teeth like snow when I bit into them. Dad put things in the microwave, but never pushed the right buttons. Mom didn't cook at all. So, I had Pop Tarts for breakfast and peanut butter and jelly sandwiches for lunch.

"Mom needs ice cream," I said and closed my eyes. "Chocolate."

"Mom needs anti-psychotics," he said. "You are her chocolate."

"I thought I was your chocolate," I said.

"You always will be, baby." He handed me a fifty-dollar bill.

"Go get your ice cream."

Dad talked about ancient turds discovered beneath sand dunes and in caves and then stared off. "Once you find those, you keep digging," he said.

I sat on the toilet, took photos of what came out. Maybe they were snowflakes and completely unique. The close-ups I'd seen at school of snowflakes were flowerish. My poop was similar to swollen caterpillars or those fat nuts that neighbors had in bowls during the holidays. I never captured the magic.

Mom called it PTSD from all the acid he'd taken. "Just so you know what to tell your therapist when you get older. He's a Pompous-Tripping-Scatological-Defect."

So instead of Dad's carcass found by a fisherman or archeologist, it was Mom, screaming down into the face of a man who put a green lava lamp in the microwave to speed up the movement of globules in one of his altered states until it exploded, scalded him with hot wax and lodged broken glass in his face and brain.

After he died, I made a collage. I found a book about weird deaths in a bookstore with great photos. One guy had testicles the size of sewer caps. Dad would have liked that. I set it up in the church on a tripod. Mom pulled it down when Grandmas and Grandpas were putting on glasses to get a closer look and the new Nebraska half-siblings, their kids, wives, and Moms took our seats and knocked us back three rows.

Death was a renaissance in our family. Dad was sure he was going to dig up mummies out there.

"Truly a success story," Mom said. "Digging up Mommy's all over Nebraska and what a cacophony of idiocy he's birthed."

Clawed relatives from the past clung like a pack of squirrel monkeys. The bark of them camped on every branch of shame, fear, and blood that perfumed my childhood. Mom stacked my gene library with night fearscapes as a kid. It wasn't creepy enough to read *Grimm's Fairytales*. Stories of people far, far away who cooked children and ate them didn't make Mom's list of bedtime tales.

Family history rattled and creaked from floorboards with groping hands and the stench of decaying lizards under my bed. It loomed and twitched from closets. No one died of heart attacks or cancer in our family. There was Aunt Nettie, who checked into a hotel room one morning, sliced her throat with a serrated knife, and left behind four kids and a husband. Uncle Ralph collected magazines. Mom said he spent his days filling out surveys to get free samples. His apartment was a hoarder's dream until a neighbor smelled something more foul than usual. The police found him suffocated underneath a magazine landslide, nude with a plastic bag over his bloated head. Grandpa Pete spent his evenings in a rocking chair in the basement whenever he got home from work.

"Used to call us down one by one," Mom said. "Not by age, so none of us knew who was next. And it wasn't to learn how to whittle wood. One day, your Grandma Betty was sitting on the steps when we got home from school. She said, 'Put down your books. You're going to the movies.' We smelled smoke, but she wouldn't let us in the house and none of us argued. She gave my older sister cash and all five of us rushed off before she changed her mind, cause she never gave us money."

You know that anticipatory fear of a train bearing down on tracks. It gets larger and larger as it moves closer and there's a moment when your body watches itself sail out just before the train hits. It was never more buoyant than when listening to Mom talk about family.

"Fire trucks, cops, and firemen everywhere with hoses and buckets, blasted out windows and char-black wood instead of a house. You ever smell tar burning?" she asked. I stared at her. I knew a response was not expected.

"It's a fever hot rubbish heap of those dead bodies your dad was always searching for. Artifacts he pretended to track were right here in our blood, baby. Right in the goddamn front yard."

"What happened next, Mom?" I asked. My body coiled in on itself, a ball of tumbleweed barreling through traffic about to get obliterated by trucks and cars. Mom's voice all husky growl, deep with cigarettes and vodka, detached from the atoms that globed this woman into matter.

"It was a hell-fire of a block party. Neighbors we'd never seen before were lined up along the sidewalks mesmerized by the flames and sizzles and glass crackling. And you could see people in that fire. Not Mom and Dad. Just faces and figures like in the clouds, except it was oranges, yellows, beautiful, and when you closed your eyes it turned into crashing waves and a thundering rainstorm. Makes sense that elements sound the same in the rage of consuming hell."

"Mom's sister, Aunt Leo, dumped us all in the back of her station wagon and drove us to her place. Lived in a house as thin as the bones of this one for the rest of our childhood. Never saw Mom or Dad again, but there was Uncle Clarence to contend with.

"Why?" I'd ask her, "why?"

"Baby," she would say, "because the world gravitates towards the ditch. At least your dad knew that. Everybody's trying to pretty up the globe with maps of continents and countries in bright colors, but you get inside the soil beneath the skin and you'll find more people popping machine guns than gum any day of the week."

I am 22 and still live in New Mexico with Mom. We have merged over the years, though I've taken to tequila while she blurs behind vodka on ice. I am weary from panic that grows inside of me. It is an unrelenting fever of anxiety that thrums through my veins. Mom races me to the hospital again and again. The ER doctor always sends psych nurses down to talk with Mom. Why doesn't she believe them? It isn't until a doctor finally puts a pacemaker in me that Mom accepts the diagnosis. A heart murmur makes more sense to her than my strange aches and nightmares, phobias of crowds and loneliness.

Mom takes me to places in Santa Fe and Taos where the caustic light beneath vigas, cut from calloused stratums of men, maintain bleeding cracks. Breasts sunken in folds like tortillas swallow these mountains. Rocks betray grounding I purport to own. Juniper and tree trunks geograph my bones, until my skin is flying off with a pack of magpies, cackling at my sockets. Circles of clouds follow me with starved eyes.

I hover around the horrid hand of my thoughts. Sometimes familial suicides, drunkards and pedophiles uncap my memory and drop from the sky like falling stars. I surrender to damp fingerprints that cover the adobe walls of me.

Mom is as feebly framed as myself. We sit in museums and watch others sway and talk as though they are convinced by the sky. Their limbs lounge like soft pillows. They don't seem to hear the drone of scuttling fingers that prod through us. Mom is one of those cracked clay pots with all the shards glued together.

"I never left you alone with your dad," she says. But, she had long been rocking in the rivers of vodka. I knew why he had so many kids. I knew how to stop breathing by the time I was eight.

Descansos are shrines to the dead. They are as rampant as sagebrush. Every few miles there is another sideshow of fake flowers, Santa, Jesus, valentines, green leprechauns, Easter bunnies, or a nativity scene with plastic animals from Party City and a fold-out tiny Christmas tree plastered with love for someone who has blasted through Jim Beam, Cuervos and Pabst. Navigating the highway with one eye open and the other squinting in prayer that the yellow line will stop gyrating is unsuccessful. Each shrine is its own condominium to a mother's grief where one of her children's vehicles became a spinning cadaver. Mom is always pointing them out when we are in the car together. "It's a great way to keep tabs on the holidays. Hearts, baby. It must be February."

"Four leaf clovers, we got to go get some green beer somewhere." Mom stops at each one so I can take a photo. "This is the only road map I will ever read," she says. I've been putting together an album for years of *Descansos*. She keeps it on the coffee table.

I drive over the Rio Grande gorge on the way to Taos. It is the one place in this state with the most suicides. 115 people have jumped off this bridge in the last 20 years. It is a landmark. I drive up here on holidays, attempt to inject my endless mullings into the merging suicidal dictionary that expands with every enterprising sap who's stood here before me. I can hear them. 'Climb up on the ledge, throw an anchor over into the depths of the bottomless crag below. Reach into the chasm in some kind of yoga pose with toes pointed and arms lifting out and up, like a 747, while you sail, down, down, down with the soundtrack to Dad's favorite album, Simon and Garfunkel's *Bridge Over Troubled Waters,* infusing the cliche.

But more is expected of our family. I am not going to be another small obit in the newspaper with an added article of myself and the crowd who jumped before me in the last 20 years. Dad's is the first demise by lava lamp recorded and I plan on making my exit unforgettable.

I hide the car behind some huge, old Cottonwood trees, so no one will find it for a few days, at least. I've been on the bridge many times. There is a box with a hotline phone in one corner with a sticker across it that says, CALL US: *WE ARE HERE TO HELP.* The bridge shakes when trucks pass over it. Gusts whirlwind.

As I walk towards it, I come up on a beauty of a *Descansos* that is all *Day of the Dead* with skeletons, blinking rainbow lights covering a juniper bush. The scent of musky wild daisies and sunflowers infuse the spectacle. These are live flowers. This person must have just died. I realize I have never photographed a fresh one. It even has balloons. I get out my cell phone to capture it to send Mom a visual goodbye. She would appreciate it, more comfortable with farewells than hellos.

I get up close and read the laminated red card within its glow.

Let's make it a duet. Happy birthday, baby.

It is in Mom's shaky handwriting. A figure stumbles out of the repetitive landscape of ragweed and cacti. This is a haunting more possessed than anything the *Grimm's brothers* ever imagined. Mom is staggering towards me. She's got two bottles and a flashlight.

I open my mouth, but winds litter sounds before words can obstruct them. It is early Fall. We are two weaving bodies inside shapeless coats. I can only follow the swaying light she holds in front of us as we step around low-lying circles of Prickly Pear patches and rocks. As we get closer to the edge it is futile to pretend we have any power. I bet at least half of these suicides wearied of fighting the forces and let themselves be taken before they were ready to jump.

We go down past the steel-grid deck and concrete and sit on the edge. This is the closest I've ever been to the 650-foot drop into the canyon and river below.

"They called this the 'bridge to nowhere,' Mom says. "For a few years they didn't have the cash to finish it." I'm clutching my half-pint of tequila taking gulps. I don't tell stories. I listen. Mom leans back and the vodka bottle attaches naturally to her lips, an extension of herself like any other limb.

"I read about a guy in Nebraska. He had a job, wife, and kids and just collapsed and died one day. When they did an autopsy they found he barely had any brain left in his skull. That's what routine and Nebraska does to a person." The air pulses. It moans through my eardrums. My boot heels are snuffed in dirt to keep the rest of me from flying off. I look at the side of Mom's face and see the nocturnal hollows of her trembling facade.

"Why are you still here?" I shout at her. "Don't you want to kill yourself?

Anyone?"

She smiles when I take her icy hand and turn it palm up, watch her as her hand naturally curls around the revolver: a snail tucking into its shell.

She looks over at me. "God, I love bone against bone, baby. It feels good." She strokes the metal. "Flesh has been exploding through history forever. The wind is a dagger: ghosting epidemics. A perpetrator knobbing open your door. Whatever, we will never go on somebody else's terms, baby."

She hurls the gun out into nothingness. An impossible distance. "At least an object will hit bottom tonight. I saw a baby stroller out there one day crusting between two boulders. Never forgot that."

She glances at me, drunk on imminent danger and ancestry. "You know I expected more of you."

I nod.

Happy birthday, baby." She smacks her bottle against mine. "You did get the only *Descansos* dedicated to a person who's still alive. That's got to mean something, right?"

The gaping wound of days unleashed themselves ahead of us. We took a long swig knowing our next stop would be the liquor store.

David Brennan

After living in Japan for 12 years David Brennan returned to Ireland in 2014. He currently lives in Cork. In 2016 he won the Frank O'Connor Mentorship Bursary Award and has been shortlisted for the Doolin Short Story Competition and the Curtis Bausse Short Story Competition. He has also published stories and poems in *Number 11*, *Memoryhouse*, *The Ogham Stone*, *Crabfat*, *Tokyo Poetry Journal* and *Jungle Crows* (a Tokyo anthology). He is currently working on a collection of stories and a novel.

Jigsaw Wabi Sabi

The keyboard lasted a week. She played it a few times and that was that. It was the same with the yoga, the long distance learning course on nutrition, the Irish Ceili classes, the belly dancing classes and the art of flower arrangement. (She didn't take too kindly to my suggestion that she check out Babeland, which offered such classes as Rope Bondage for Beginners, The Art of the Blow Job and Get Knottier: Even More Rope Bondage.) What she really wanted was a baby. But I was scared the same thing might happen with the baby. And besides I didn't really want a baby – I was far too obsessed with myself. I had quit my job at Cork English School and was determined to become a full-time writer. She worked at Cork's Apple headquarters', bringing in enough money to sustain us both. What she did exactly I didn't know, except that she was part of a team. She asked her grandmother for advice when there was trouble. Her grandmother had been dead five years.

Grandmothers scared me. My own believed I was possessed after an incident when I was just seven: I killed two of her hens on a visit to her farm. I guess it was an instinct thing. I saw the fuckers running, picked up a crowbar, chased after them and dropped the crowbar on one and then the other. My grandmother doused me in holy water and shouted curses over me. This incident tainted her view of me for the rest of her days.

So when the thousand-piece jigsaws came along I suspected it was another fad. She opened the first one Saturday morning – a picture of the Titanic. I drove back to my hometown alone. We were going through difficult times and a bit of space can work wonders. When I came back Sunday evening the Titanic was complete after a twelve-hour struggle.

> *Sadako Sasaki folded 644 paper cranes before she became too weak to fold anymore and died on October 25, 1955. She had been a baby when the Hiroshima bomb went off and was exposed to radiation, which led to her developing leukemia. An ancient Japanese legend promises that anyone who folds a thousand origami cranes will be granted a wish by the gods. Or in other variations you'll be granted recovery from illness or injury. But there's a catch: The thousand cranes have to be completed in a year. The crane in Japan is one of the mystical or holy creatures (others include the dragon and the tortoise) and is said to live for a thousand years. Her classmates completed the rest after she died.*

She was born in the city of Yokohama in 1987. We'd dated for years before getting married. All that getting married idea was hers. We'd met in Japan at the school where I taught. These teacher student roles tended to flip over the years. She continued with the jigsaws and, once completed, she framed them and hung them on the walls: Machu Picchu, a street scene of Dickensian London, Starry Night and so on.

'How do you even approach it,' I asked?

'Doesn't matter,' she said.

'Where do you start,' I asked? 'Do you build it one piece at a time or do you look at the big picture and try to follow that. Or do you select one piece, one corner and focus on that?'

'You start at the end, of course, and work your way inwards.'

'Do you not feel like giving up sometimes?'

'No,' she said.

'Why?'

'I wouldn't start if I didn't know I could finish.'

'Like Columbus?'

'Who?'

She craved stability; a house, kids and a normal life, while I craved travel, adventure, other women and foolishness, even though I was limping towards forty with a banjaxed foot, knee and back. I should have been happy to settle down with a beautiful, kind woman ten years my younger. Following your dream isn't all it's cracked up to be. You know; the no money, the lack of options, the sacrifices, the sitting in cafés for endless hours typing away – wondering if you've got talent or if you've got some kind of disease. Sometimes she got that – sometimes she didn't. I couldn't and didn't blame her – well I did. We blamed each other for the mess we were in. If one of us had walked away years ago it would have been much easier. We would have gotten divorced only we'd just gotten married. What would the family say?

Instead of her interest waning, the opposite happened. Every spare moment she had, she sat at the table fiddling with the pieces. At first I welcomed the change as I could spend guilt-free time on my writing projects. I didn't have to take her for a drive on Sundays. She stopped cleaning the house and cooking; a turn of events which caused me great distress and although I fought my corner she appeared as a woman possessed. She'd come home from work and immediately launch into whatever puzzle she was working on. Our already sparse communication deteriorated into bare functionary utterances and it was almost as if we had our own private language of grunts and moans. She started to stay up late – to lose sleep, and to neglect all things besides the jumbling of jigsaw pieces. At first she selected them randomly but was soon doing them by theme. She'd spend a week doing Animals of the Serengeti then move on to Modern Architectural Structures.

Entire weekends were now spent crouched over the table madly constructing, fixing, pulling and weaving. She resembled a spider on speed or at times an angel spinning silk. Her condition worsened though her skill increased. A puzzle that had taken her twelve-hours now only took her six. Concerned she was losing her mind, I recommended she go see a psychologist. I thought at first she was escaping from the reality of our broken love, but when I noticed she was turning out three a day I realized she was going for the thousand. If she pumped out a thousand in a year she could have whatever she wanted – most likely my head on a plate (in the form of me being hit by a truck or something like that). I wasn't exactly sure what she would be wishing, but I was fairly fucking sure it would have something to do with me and that her grandmother was involved – perhaps mine too.

> *Sadako was at home with her mother and grandmother when the explosion occurred about two kilometers away from ground zero. She was blown out the window and her mother ran out to find her two-year-old daughter alive with no apparent injuries. While they were fleeing, Sadako and her mother were caught in black rain. Her grandmother rushed back to the house but was never seen again.*

Why would you bother making a jigsaw? I understand it's a puzzle to be solved. I understand there must be satisfaction in its completion. But what do you do with it afterwards. Hang it on the wall? Why not just buy a painting?

The small apartment filled with jigsaws. The walls disappeared.

The real trouble began when she started to get into *Wabi Sabi*.

'Wasabi – The green shit you put on the sushi?'

'No, Wabi Sabi...IRISH' she said, as she clicked her tongue and cast her eyes upwards.

What the fuck is she on about now, I thought.

I'd walked in on her and she had a hammer in her hand and a finished puzzle of Nemo, that fish all the other fish are trying to find. She had the puzzle balanced above the table by two pillars of books. My books. After she completed the jigsaws she glued them and left them to set for a day, ensuring that they could take certain Wabi Sabi practices. She took one swing of the hammer and then laid it gently in the table, stepped back and contemplated the impact – a hole right through Nemo's head.

'Nice,' she said. 'Wabi Sabi.'

'Mind my fucking books, will yeah? Fuck sake, you've no respect for my things,' I said, making sure I stepped out of reach of the arch of the if-swung hammer.

I read up about the Wabi Sabi shit. Although difficult to define, in short it's finding beauty in imperfection, in earthiness. Zen. Words are useless.

Wabi Sabi: Wabi Sabi...

So she'd stand back and fuck a raw egg at a finished puzzle of Mother Theresa, Genghis Khan, or some in-the-news politician, then she'd get the hair dryer and start solidifying the chaotic paths the unborn chicken had taken. Or she'd staple a small shopping list over a puzzle of the lower Manhattan financial district.

It was soon after this Wabi Sabi breakthrough that she started to sell the puzzles. She quit her job. The money she got wasn't enough though, and I had to start working so that we could pay the rent. I picked up part-time work landscaping and I wrote whenever I could. Talk of divorce abated. She started to do shows. I know it sounds ridiculous, but people were willing to pay to watch her moving Jigsaw pieces. There's a weekly event in Cork at an artists café where unusual acts take to the stage. She got a thirty-minute slot. They watched in complete silence and then loudly applauded after she'd finished. Can you believe it? Of course the skimpy dress she wore helped focus their attention. You should have seen the other acts. There was a woman who sat there with a sewing machine and made ribbons... She'd recently had a baby. For the finale she slipped her right breast out and squirted a little milk on the ribbon; then tied the ribbon in her hair – an act which was greeted with rapturous applause. And then there were the poets... I'd rather eat a raw turnip (a full-sized one) than listen to more mystical Irish shit. These weren't just your normal run of the mill, smelly, haven't-showered-in-two-week poets, with beards down to their bellybutton. No among their rank there were: Oisin Venison who held the Irish record for being on the dole for the longest consecutive stretch: 22 years and counting; Cormac O'Braonan who not only composed exclusively in Gaelic but he refused to even speak English; Philly Allen who read pages from the phonebook as his mate Sick Pete made background animal noises.

It didn't stop there. No – she started to get famous. A YouTube video that went viral. She became known as the *Japanese Jigsaw Genius*. It wasn't just the speed and dexterity she exhibited which drew attention, but the Wabi Sabi dimension, which attracted the gaze of some of the heavies in the art scene. There were interviews in magazines and newspapers. She stayed out longer after her events. I noticed she dressed up – paid more attention to her appearance. I suspected liaisons, but she swore she was faithful. She now initiated sex. She suggested we both take the Rope Bondage for Beginners class. We signed up, but I, due to fear, pulled out on the night of the first class and she ended up going alone, furthering my suspicions that something was afoot. The idea of it had been much more attractive than the reality.

I too had my success, but not as I envisaged. As she changed it seemed I changed. As the months went on I lost interest in my writing projects and even had faint longings of starting a family. I'd always loved nature and I'd always felt more comfortable outside than inside so the landscaping job was perfect for me. Meanwhile she grew more and more obsessed with her work. For whole days she would remain indoors working on her creations. I now took on full household duties including cooking.

One weekend she ran out of puzzles and was in serious distress. Rather than endure her constant whining I drove her to Dublin Sunday morning where there was a store open. On the three-hour trip back to Cork she completed a Jackson Pollock portrait. Now fuck me, imagine trying to figure that shit out. I was just glad of the silence.

She befriended artists, musicians, and other degenerates. When she agreed to the threesomes I had always envisaged I felt disgusted and disappointed.

Remarkably, she hit the 1000 a month before the year expired and then almost on cue she announced she was pregnant. The deal was complete. The months passed and Noriko arrived healthy and beautiful. Yes, she was mine – I could tell. Her sweat with its unmistakable pungent odour could only come from Finn DNA; redolent of my father, my brothers and I. She was all I cared about and I guess I started to understand why my wife and I had endured each other for so long.

Last week we were on the Late-Late show. We'd decide to make a weekend of it and booked a hotel for two nights in Dublin. So, there I was in the audience holding the baby – wearing one of those baby holders. 'Ladies and gentlemen please welcome the Japanese woman currently taking the art world by storm – the *Japanese Jigsaw Genius.*'

The applause-guy jumped up waving his hands wildly like we were retards and didn't know when to clap.

We clapped.

She looked so hot dressed in that black one piece. I couldn't believe she was my wife. Ryan thought she was hot too. He was practically drooling all over her on national television.

'And if I may ask how do you get your inspiration,' he asked, reaching over and touching her hand. Cunt. Twenty minutes into the interview and I was finally expecting some kind of a mention.

'My grandmother,' she said.

She proceeded to tell him about their relationship and how she still communicated with her. In Japan it's common to believe that your ancestors are still in contact with and protecting you. Ryan asked for an example and she tells him she was going to get divorced but her grandmother advised her to give it another try. Thanks, thanks a fucking million I said casting my eyes looking up at the lights, which were roasting us.

'Fascinating,' said the cunt. 'Absolutely fascinating, and I believe he's here tonight.' The applause guy jumped up again. I felt grateful for my landscaping job.

The camera shot to me.

'What's it like being a house-hubby,' Ryan asked, placing unnatural stress on the *house-hubby* like he was speaking to a child.

'Go fuck yourself,' I said.

No, I didn't, but I should have. I think I came across like a fucking eejit as the nerves were eating me up.

He invited her to a party that night. She said it was important for publicity; there would be a lot of important people there.

He's harmless, she said.

He's got a dick and money, I said.

He's not handsome, she said. He's kinda like Woody in Toy Story.

I know she likes Woody in Toy Story.

She says I'm paranoid.

I've finally started to piss sitting down which has resulted in a massive reduction in the number of fights. Plus, we just don't have the energy we once had for the fighting. Noriko makes me happy. She reminds me how lucky we are to be born in this time and age.

When Sadako Sasaki was eleven she stared to develop swellings on her neck and behind her ears. Diagnosed with acute malignant lymph gland leukemia she was hospitalized and given a year to live. While in hospital she learned of the legend of the cranes from a friend who was also hospitalized with 'atom bomb disease,' as her mother called it. Towards the end, after numerous attempts by her family to urge her to eat, she requested rice tea and remarked it was tasty. She died a few minutes later.

Balancing the part-time landscaping and the housework keeps me busy.

I'm good at it – this house-hubby stuff. Perhaps it's what I was born to do. I have to believe that, otherwise... She's in New York now at an artist conference and will meet with Yoko Ono amongst others. We've another baby on the way. So here I am – in Fitzgerald Park, by the Lee, with some of the other house-hubbies drinking in the oxygen as hordes of kids run hither and thither over the grass. Their movements appear to me not dissimilar to the laws governing the dynamics of a brood of hens. We have a bit of craic sometimes. We go out for drinks when the wives allow us. And I'm still writing whenever I can get time. I had a story published last week in a journal in America. That keeps me going.

Just past a turn in the Lee, under the shadow of the infamous abandoned mental home, a large grey crane lands on the bank. He appears to be looking at me and then nodding towards the sinister, imposing, boarded-up, red-bricked St. Kevin's. He does this three times. I must be losing my fucking mind, I'm thinking, as I stare back at it in disbelief, until Noriko comes running over crying and breaks me out of my trance. Look at the crane, I say in an attempt to divert her attention, but when I look up it's gone. I wonder sometimes whether I am going mad. I hear two voices – one loud and the other more cautious, more gentle, almost imperceptible. One of the voices says to be patient, to endure and to wait, while the other whispers to run, and to keep on running.

Emily Brewin

Emily Brewin is an Australian writer and educator. Her first novel, *Hello, Goodbye,* was released in June this year with Allen and Unwin. She has been awarded an Australian Society of Authors Emerging Writers' and Illustrators' Mentorship for her fiction writing. Her short stories have been shortlisted for a number of literary awards, including the Alan Marshall Short Story Award, Overland's Fair Australia Prize and the Elyne Mitchell Writing Awards. Her second novel is due for release with Allen and Unwin in July 2018. She is currently working on her third.

Road Trips and Fairy Tales

My face was already damp with sweat when I woke. It was going to be a stinker. The type of day that was perfect for frying an egg on the bonnet of our yellow Valiant. If Dad were around, I might ask if we could try it, but he always left for work while I was still asleep.

A thudding sound nearby roused me from bed and I wandered out to the kitchen where some vegemite toast curled on a plate on the table.

'Surprise', my mother bustled into the room carrying two blue suitcases, bangles clanging up her arm. 'How'd you like to take a break?'

I sat down, my head foggy with sleep and squinted at her.

'A holiday', she said with a half formed smile.

I stared at the plate and asked, 'What about school?'

She put the cases down, and reached up to the kitchen cupboard above the fridge to an old jam jar where the housekeeping money was kept. Dad put it in there on payday each week, taking his time, as Mum's eyes darted towards it. After, she would tip the contents on the bench and count it while he watched the telly. If it were short, she'd huff and bang around the kitchen so he'd have to turn the volume up.

She used it for groceries then bought ugly fabric leftovers to make me clothes, with the change. Some nights from bed, I'd hear her asking for more. The whine in her voice made my teeth clench, and I was glad when

Dad said no. I hated her fabric creations.

'It's almost the holidays. An extra week won't hurt', she said, turning back to the bench so quickly her wrap-around skirt swished at her ankles. She emptied the jar and stuffed the notes into her tasselled handbag, leaving a few silver coins behind.

'And Dad?'

'He's working with Uncle Brett all week. Plus, you know how much he hates travelling' She smiled so her face lit up and the semi-circles beneath her eyes disappeared, and told me to get dressed quick-sticks.

Finally, excitement swelled in my chest. I loved long car trips, sticky icy-poles in the back seat and driving with the window down. The open road. Freedom from school and chores, and wondering if Dad would come home after work.

Mum chucked the suitcases in the boot while I climbed into the back and felt the purr of our Valiant beneath me. She reversed roughly down the driveway and soon I was watching the houses in our street slip by. Then school, where my best mate, Lily, would be waiting for me.

We sped out of town. I laughed when Mum whooped then turned to look out the back window at the *Mildura – Mallee Region* sign getting smaller and smaller before disappearing altogether.

It wasn't long until endless brown paddocks dotted with sheep stretched as far as my eyes could see and the stash of butterscotch drops Mum had given me ran dry. When I finally thought to ask where we were going, her eyes drifted to the rear view mirror and away again.

'The beach.'

I bounced up and down, and wished I'd put my cossie on before we left. 'How long till we get there.'

'A few days', her eyes drifted again.

'Huh?' I stopped bouncing.

'You'll love it, Iz', she jumped in as if anticipating my surprise. 'A woman from pottery class told me about this town, not far from Brisbane, where people do yoga on the beach and live in little shacks in the rainforest.' Her voice got shrill, the way it did when she was anxious or over-excited or both.

It made me nervous.

'Lots of artists go there.'

I shrunk a little at *artist* and sucked on some loose hair. It tasted like Dad's shaving soap. I washed myself with it sometimes because I liked the way he smelt. In our house, *artist* was a loaded word. When I started school, Mum turned the garden shed at the bottom of our yard into a 'studio' and bought a second hand pottery wheel. It was dark and cool in there, and smelt like incense. Her crooked creations lined the shelves and sat awkwardly on the windowsill. Dad wouldn't let them in the house.

'Is that the real reason why Dad's not coming?'

'Mmmm', she nodded slightly so her dangly earrings swayed.

I looked out the window and imagined Dad in his singlet, helping Uncle Brett pour concrete at the new estate on the edge of town. It was just one of the jobs he did, like working at the racecourse and mowing lawns for rich people. After work, he'd go to the pub and stay there till dinnertime. I wondered what he'd eat when he got home and discovered Mum hadn't left him anything. He won't be happy.

When I got sick of looking out the car window, I dragged my book of fairy tales out from under the seat. It was babyish, I knew, but I didn't care. At night, when Dad came home smelling of beer and Mum stormed a path to the door to ask where he'd been, I'd slip under my bedcovers and read it, losing myself in it's thick white pages while my parents argued.

I didn't look up from my book until we pulled into a roadside motel with a sign that flashed 'vacant' out front. It was too dark to make out the rest of the town but I had just finished The Pied Piper of Hamelin and imagined it as a crooked little village. When Mum said it was the 'arse end of nowhere', I imagined something else.

She gave the fat sweaty bloke at the motel counter a big smile, but didn't answer when he asked where we came from. He grinned in return then offered us some free videos from the office out back. Something about the way he looked at Mum made me yelp, 'no'.

The flashing sign shone pink through the saggy curtains of our room and onto Mum's face. She exhaled loudly as she sat down on the end of the bed. Suddenly, her sparkle was gone and the wrap-around skirt tangled at her ankles. I hated the way she got old when no one but me was watching.

She unwrapped a couple of biscuits from the small wicker basket on the coffee table when I said I was hungry, so I knew not to bother asking to call Dad.

When she undressed and climbed under the thin sheet beside me, I wrapped my legs around hers and read her a story, Beauty and the Beast. It reminded me of her and Dad, and the yelling that got so bad some nights even the book couldn't distract me. I'd stare at the ceiling and listen to Dad go on about 'hard work' and 'putting food on the table', and Mum complaining she could hardly 'breathe'.

When she said, she wanted to work again; Dad laughed and asked what she planned to do. I wondered why she never said pottery. I wanted her desperately to take Dad to the shed, to show him how good she was getting; how her bowls no longer sagged at the sides and how the cup handles stayed straight. I thought of the Beast, and wished Dad would transform before her eyes.

We left the motel as the sun came up, stopping later for bacon and eggs at a truckies rest. The drive that day was longer, hotter and even more boring than the one before. We travelled inland through towns with funny names like Dubbo and Dunedoo. When my jumbo pack of salt and vinegar chips ran out, and I got sick of reading, I counted the passing cars instead, always keeping an eye out for a Holden like Dad's.

Mum listened to the radio, singing loudly when her favourite song came on, the one about being a dreamer and not the only one. It scared me the way she disappeared into things, like songs and pottery. The way her eyes got dreamy and she floated away despite being in the front seat.

At home, she spent more and more time in the shed, slipping away straight after dinner to spin her creations. She looked different when she emerged late at night, shiny and happy and far, far away.

If Dad were home, he'd watch telly in the family room, laughing loudly at Ossie Ostrich while I curled up on his lap and listened to his heartbeat.

That night, we stayed at another brown brick motel with flashing lights. This time there was a lady out front with fairy floss hair and a permanent frown. She wouldn't give us a discount when Mum asked, and said we'd better be out by 9am. This time, Mum's smile slipped before we got to our room and the blue suitcases seemed heavier in her hands.

I read her Jack and the Beanstalk in bed because Dad always told her money didn't grow on trees. In the story it did, well at the top of one. The beanstalk led to pots of treasure and a goose that lay golden eggs. Sometimes, Dad promised we'd be rich one day. He said he'd buy us a house and Mum a new car, which made her stare blankly out the kitchen window.

When she closed her eyes and started to snore softly, I stopped reading. Then I turned off the light and listened to cicadas singing outside.

The next day, I spent most of the trip lying across the back seat. If I stretched, my head hit one door while my feet nudged the other. I dipped in and out of sleep, waking to go to the toilet and to eat the punnet of strawberries Mum had bought from a makeshift shop on the side of the road.

'Not long now', she called, glancing back at me through her big round sunnies, her face bright again.

I sat up.

'Look, the Clarence River', she continued, knuckles white against the wheel as if she was afraid to let it go.

We passed a sign that said *Welcome to the town of Grafton*.

I wanted to stop and move my legs, but Mum said I'd have to wait. It made me cross. I was queasy from the fruit and from being stuck in the hot car for three days. I wanted to run for a while, maybe go for a dip in the river, and call Dad. I wanted to tell him about the motels we'd stayed in and about the monster trucks that flew past, making our car rock.

'My legs hurt.'

'Just a couple more hours', she said without glancing around.

'That's ages. I want to stop now.'

'I said, no!' Her knuckles got whiter.

It made me angry, the way we always did what she wanted to do. Dad was right. She was selfish.

'I want, Dad.' I'd wanted to say it for two days but something always stopped me, the careful way she walked to the hotel reception desks or her pasted on smile. I was scared of upsetting her. Dad upset her.

'Iz...' she petered out and kept driving.

'No!' I yelled, filling with indignation. 'It's always about you. You. You. You.'

Her shoulders tensed.

I leaned forward, close to her ear. 'You!'

It was what Dad said on the nights he got home late from the pub; and stuffed into the back seat of our overheated Valiant, I knew it was true. Dad worked hard and Mum did nothing important. He brought home the bacon.

I snorted. If she worked, she might have been able to afford the ice cream I'd asked for at the last stop.

'Be quiet, Izzy.' It was a warning. I sat back and grinned smugly out the window. I knew how to hurt her.

But she was used to being hurt. The night before we left, I'd watched them through the gap beside my bedroom door. Dad unsteady on his feet as if he might fall, smiling at Mum, who was shouting at him for spending the grocery money on drink again.

'How am I supposed to feed us?'

'Not my problem', he shrugged. 'I work, *you* sort out the rest.'

I opened my door a little further.

Mum shook her head, small in front of Dad, until she spoke. 'I hate you', her voice was like gravel, 'and this stifling bloody life.'

There was silence worse than the yelling.

Then Dad's hand cracked against her face, dropping quickly to his side again as if it had never lifted in the first place. He pushed past her into the kitchen. I heard the fridge door open.

Mum held a hand to her cheek. It made me want to cry out in fear, because he'd hit her but also because she wanted something more than what she had, and where did that leave me.

We drove the next two hours without talking, the hot wind whistling through the window, Mum's cheeks flushed with it or with something else... it was hard to tell.

Eventually, we arrived in another town. 'We're here', she announced as the ocean twinkled through a row of palms on the side of the road. 'Byron Bay.' Then she grinned at me in the rear view mirror until my anger faded.

She chatted happily, as we drove past shops with wind chimes and houses with stained glass windows. It reminded me of the way she was when she emerged from her pottery shed, all new and hopeful. I couldn't wait to run across the hot sand to the water. Seeing it, made me sorry for my friends in school still and for Dad pouring concrete with Uncle Brett.

We pulled into a petrol station so Mum could ask directions to the caravan park. She found fifty cents on the ground outside and gave it to me with a hug, telling me to go and get the ice cream I wanted.

The little bells on her skirt tinkled as she walked to the counter, head held high. It filled me with happiness, like when she'd sit on Dad's lap and tweak the end of his nose. If Mum could be happy here, maybe Dad could be too. They could be happy together.

The fifty-cent piece pressed roughly in my hand as I walked to the fridge. Beyond it was an orange pay phone, tucked in beside the bread shelf at the back of the store. Fairy tales always had happy endings. I tried not to look at the ice creams as I made a beeline for the phone and dropped my coin in the slot. Then, I dialled our number.

Dad picked up straight away.

'It's me', I blurted out.

The phone line buzzed softly.

'Dad?'

'Where are you?' He drew the words out slowly.

I checked Mum. Her back was turned and she was chatting to the man behind the counter.

'Byron Bay', I told him. 'We're staying at the caravan park near the beach.'

No response. For a moment, I thought he'd hung up on me.

'Right', he said finally. 'Don't tell your mother, but I'll see you soon.'

Clementine Ewokolo Burnley

Clementine Ewokolo Burnley writes, works as an organiser in communities of colour, and meditates. Born in Cameroon, raised in Cameroon and the UK, Clementine now lives and writes between lots of different places. You can find her at https://about.me/clementine.ewokolo.burnley or on Twitter at @decolonialheart

A Place Called Out

It is well before dawn. Big Ma is tugging at my toes. She does this every morning, standing back light-footed when I kick out, pretending to be angry. I make sure to miss today. For a while Big Ma has been heavy-footed and slow. She opens my bedroom curtains to let in the early morning breeze, then goes into the little parlour where we also eat our meals. She lays my white robe out on the sofa. There are white plastic slippers, still in a see-through bag, and a white cloth for my head.

As she eases into her armchair, placing a cushion where the loose spring would otherwise poke into her back, she says,

"Go and wash, little mother." She looks exhausted all of a sudden.

I wait for her to continue, uncertain if she means to say more but she waves me away. The water is turned off at the pumping station overnight to save power. So, we ration it out in buckets that stand in a neat row in the bathroom and in the kitchen. Big Ma will not let me light a fire in case I burn myself like Amma our neighbour, whose kerosene stove exploded and set her clothes on fire. Amma has ropy silver gray scars that coil around her neck like jewellery and disappear under her clothes.

I have watched Big Ma set the fire in our iron stove often enough. She feeds the slowly reddening coals with slivers of dry wood. All the while she blows steadily until live flames jump and bigger pieces of wood blaze up to send the water in the aluminium kettle hissing through the spout in ecstasies of steam. This morning I check hopefully, as I have for the past four mornings. The coals in the stove are grey, covered in a layer of cold ash. This morning too I give up on my dream of hot water.

It's early in the day and so, even here on the equator the bathroom feels cool. The bucket is half empty. Three bowls full, if I am careful. I stand on the wooden slats of the washing platform inside the shower cubicle, scoop up the first bowl and test the temperature with my finger. I already know the water is cold.

"Bad luck!" I say to myself, emphatically but not very loud.

Dipping my hands in the water, I work up a lather by rubbing my palms briskly together. I rinse the soap into the bowl and scoop it up with my washcloth. I work the wet cloth across my rounded belly and rinse it off with the second bowl of water. My back is dry. Big Ma always checks the middle of my spine to see if I have poured the water over my whole body. I stand on my tiptoes, hold my breath and pour the water, screaming as it follows the hollow curve of my spine.

When I come out of the bathroom Big Ma's eyes are closed. She is breathing heavily, arm hanging over the side of the chair. I shake her.

"Big Ma, I am going soon."

She used to always ask, "Where?"

I wait to answer, "Out."

Big Ma opens her eyes and smiles at the wall opposite. She's supposed to say

"A place called Out? I didn't know there such a place." The first time I said this she laughed unexpectedly, the sound cracking from a wide-open mouth. This time she does not ask, and I say nothing to her.

Instead, while getting dressed I tell the black and white photo of my mother in its wooden frame on the wall of my room.

"Mami Wota is for old women. Yes, you with the eyes as innocent as the dairy cows on Mount Cameroon. You at university in Derby; your goddess has not protected us." I say it so low I am sure Big Ma does not hear me. Then I finish getting dressed, shut the door behind me and walk to the river.

When the adults in the small neighborhood turn their lips downwards and waggle disapproving fingers, Big Ma translates my not being like a girl into faster, smarter, stronger, better than other girls. Which is what she has wanted all along. Other girls strain their eyesight to pick tiny bits of gravel out of the low quality rice their parents get from the local market. With the money my mother sends, Big Ma buys Uncle Ben's long grain American rice in a cardboard box from the air-conditioned supermarket. Instead of picking rice I spend whole afternoons anchored by skinny brown legs from the branches of cashew trees, reading thick books and pelting the neighborhood boys with unripe fruit. In my head I am already at boarding school in an Enid Blyton novel. In reality the local Mission school is my best chance at the sort of "A" level results I want.

The meeting place is just where the Jenngellay river settles into a slow-moving, u- shaped curve. I know this spot well. Big Ma and I have lived an easy half-hour walk from the Jenngellay all my life. My toes know the slow suck-release of yellow river mud. I love to catch gray shrimp while Big Ma gathers herbs for the shrine in her bedroom. If I change my mind I could be sitting on my grandmother's lap by sunrise. But my mind is made up. The seeds of stubbornness Big Ma watered have flowered into something her Mami Wota did not predict. So I wait under the Ombay bridge in the half-light, turning every sound into the plap-plap sound of Esango's hurrying footsteps, or area boys stalking girls through the brush, or Big Ma making her way to stop me.

The time passes slowly enough for me to take the plastic flip-flops off and find a small stick with which I poke into the holes that surround me. There are many land crabs in the sandbanks. When the other children arrive with their parents at full light, most stare curiously at the muddy stick and my wet feet. Esango comes last of all. He gives no explanation for his lateness but seems embarrassed.

By now the sun has been up for an hour and the weaver birds are starting to tire. The violent heat sucks the energy out of their cheeky morning calls. The birds interrupt each other in a cacophony of song, each call overlaying the other, forming a solid carpet of sound that makes it pointless to speak. So we are standing on the bank of the Jenngellay river, waiting silently for our turn in the water with Esango. At thirteen, I am the youngest in the line of solemn children. We are arranged in order of age, with me at the end.

The swelling darkness of my body is hidden by a loose-fitting dress. My short-cropped black curls are covered by my white headwrap. I have tied it inexpertly and it is starting to unravel. None of this is what I would wear by choice. Still, I begged Big Ma for months before she harrumphed at my foolishness and agreed, first to buy the lengths of white cloth, and then to take me to the tailor in the market.

I prefer not to go back to the office where in place of an interview, a thick-bellied man had polished my neck with a clammy tongue, before rolling my nipple between his fingertips. I will not marry an "Office Oga" and raise his child. The boldest of the palm oil-yellow birds continue to flit down to the water. They jump in one at a time to emerge dancing and shaking violently. Each bird keeps one white-rimmed eye fixed on us. I think of Ham staring at his father Noah's naked body.

Esango talks in the steady tone I have grown to know well over the last twelve weeks. I nod at intervals, even though I cannot follow what he is saying. I have been watching the birds for hours, while waiting for my turn in the water. This weaver bird lifts off the ground. It is shaking, wings folding open and shut in a slow, jerky motion I have not seen before. There is a black cord tethering the weaver bird to the ground. It lashes back and forth. The weaver bird's eyes are fixed. One is punctured, covering its cheek in a sticky liquid. The cord writhes and comes to rest on the ground, revealing a black snake coiled tight around the unmoving bird.

On the outside I look normal. I can tell because Esango is still speaking, gesturing occasionally with his hands. He is looking at me with a perfectly straight face, as I walk to where he waits in the water. If my belly were growing, stretching out to the stars he would notice and stop talking. I hold on to his voice, which sounds reassuringly calm.

Esango stops me, gesturing with his hand out flat. Grasping my shoulders, he turns me so I am facing away from him. The people on the riverbank are nodding with me, as I go down into the river for the first time. The water completely covers me. I come up, blinking and open my eyes, though they begin to sting. Flat on my back, I notice the sky over his shoulder is gray with thunderheads. How dark the sky, I am thinking, when the whole horizon tilts crazily, but really I know I am moving, tipping over flat on my back, the smell of damp wool in my nose as Esango leans over me. His face is serious. His bare feet are planted firm on the river bottom, toes pressing into the mud. In this spot, standing upright, the water that only touches the tops of Esango's thighs, is above my hips. I am holding his wrist, my fingers clenched hard around it. Last night I practised holding my breath, then breathing deeply, sucking the air into my lungs. Mouth shut, eyes shut – or open if I did not mind eyes red as kola nut for hours afterwards.

Esango's arm cradles my back, his hand grasping my arm close to the elbow. It feels firm but relaxed, I think, as my face breaks the surface of the moving water. The water is unexpectedly cold against my spine. It occurs to me that there was no need for the third bowl of water this morning. The bridge overhead is crowded with curious faces.

Maybe Big Ma is there watching. My legs float up to the surface. My face feels twisted, eyes opening for an instant to shut tight against the water streaming down to my chin. I take a deep breath, lips pressed into a flat line, as I go over on my back again. My fragile calm is dissolving. I have always been a little afraid of the rushing river, quiet as it is in this particular spot. Jenngellay is devious and deep further along, with unexpected rapids and outcrops of slippery rock, jagged edges gleaming.

I am tugging at Esango's sleeve and he frowns, glancing at the bundle of pleated cloth in my hand. My knuckles are bulging with the force I am exerting. I am holding on tight enough to hurt. His surplice will be wrinkled by the end of the morning. The starch of the shirt he is wearing, is already wilted, the collar hanging down like a dispirited grey parrot.

The choirboys are stamping, hop hopping and staring down at the blades of elephant grass, hammered flat by the feet of the crowd on the riverbank. There are fire ants in the grass. The choir begins to sing "Washed by the Blood of the Lamb". The less dedicated Christians are now openly slapping at ankles and legs where the ants sense a stampede could be imminent.

The words come to me through the water and I think, it's so noisy the last of the weaverbirds must have flown by now. The tears wash away. Esango does not notice. He is smiling and shaking us by the hand again one after the other. There is a sticky wetness on my knee. When my hands come away bloody I think I didn't fall, but there is no cut when I wipe the skin clean and then it is running down my legs. And suddenly I have a future again.

Paul Duffy

Paul Duffy is a native of Dublin and has lived for extended periods in the west of Ireland, the south of France and in Western Australia. He has had stories published in the *Irish Times*, in the journal *Causeway/Cabhsair* and broadcast on RTÉ Radio 1. He has been shortlisted for a number of awards, winning in 2015, the Over the Edge award for his story *Redolence*. Paul also regularly publishes in both English and French on the subjects of medieval history and archaeology. He lives with his family in the Wicklow Mountains and works as an archaeologist.

Voltage

Smoke deep and with intent in the waste scrub by the train station. Smoke diesel-tinged resin through a crushed coke can stabbed with pocket-knife holes. Smoke danger into the safe suburban streets. Hold the naphtha hot breath. Ignore the sear and melt of alveoli. Mannish disregard for that. Quell the sick feeling with the metallic slug of brandless pilsner. Walk along surfaces. Through the poorly drained concrete lanes backed with unused garages. Walk along the tree-root busted path and the shopping centre tarmac bejewelled with glinting diamonds of carglass, over the low kerb wall and across a road made of squares of ribbed concrete sealed with tubular squirms of black tar. Head for the margins, three abreast and hoods up. Your mothers left indoors and the other doors full of other fuckers mothers who are part of the stonewall gaze, the cold facade, the impenetrable lockout of a suburb at dusk. Walk between the joins of the estate. Dark descending with the stars lighting up in bunches over the wires of the train line and the broken floodlights of the tennis court.

Breathe the dull smoky red skyline and absorb the full-lunged damp power of it. Walk onwards to the graveyard wall that was here long before the houses came up flush with it. Organic stone on stone repointed crassly with council cement. Vault and land with the confidence of a stride barely broken. Don't talk, just continue the road. Follow the track that needs no acknowledgement up to the leeside of the ruined church. Iron bars in the shattered walls and inconceivably old graffiti clinging somehow to the sandstone, spelling names of long forgotten thrash bands that must have been revered by the first ever kids to own this estate. Or before even when the sprawl stopped fields back to the west and they came stomping out here in the dusk in cutsleeve shirts and laced up boots to smoke and spit and sniff glue like men and venerate Dark Angel, Kreator, Corrosion of Conformity. Stop in the shadow of the wall, wrestle a joint into being and drink another can from the bag looking out over the dirty expanse of the bay, the strewn emptiness and braided channels and mudflats left behind by the egress of thousands of cubic tons of seawater dragged off to some distant shore. Consider the invisible immense net of gravity, the blurred out moon clawing its dues but don't speak of these things yet. Drink and smoke and laugh lightness. Kick the hummocky sandy scraw, oblivious to the jags of crockery, the coffin nails and knuckle bones breaking the surface in a thousand tiny extrusions. Drink the energy, the rawness, the possibility of the night and forge on across the coast road with the yellow effluent of light disgorging from the streetlamps ticking on along the grand arc of the bay. Chew on the seawrack smell, the algae zest and mollusc and lugworm churned sands. Follow the bay seawards and descend down at the appointed place onto the foreshore and forge on through the shingle of dogwhelk and the knotted fists of seaweed and the humped banks of vomited bladderwrack. Slog along the back gardens of the rich houses with their gardens running down to the shore, their boundaries of full rhododendron, buddleia, ortensia, chickenwire and driftwood driven palisades. Pass deep in the rhythm of your work, crunching draining steps, hoods down, the shush of the sea away to your right and the moon suddenly large and lounging in a bank of oily cloud. Grip cans of beer in your sleeve sheathed hands, the convection numbing fingers – you have all mastered the slug and stride like men. Walk with entitlement, with mustered menace, with the righteousness of coming from over the tracks. From smaller houses fitted closer together.

Reach the place. Push in the chainlink fence close to the rusted post. Bull in through the bushes. Retrace the steps of two weeks previous. Up the overgrown curving way between the ewe and alder, past the massive pampas grass in the lawn. Past the glasshouse where you came that first night, egging each other on, quietly undoing the latch and drinking inside in the darkness and in restrained quiet as the rain burst itself on the corrugated glass panes and you lay down along the desiccated leaf litter of dead tomato and courgette plants and filled the place with silvery smoke, feeling the cold seep into your kidneys and eyeing her occasionally and stretching out antennae, filtering her speak from the low babble and the slight, tinny sounds from the Walkman turned up full playing Mudhoney. Alive to the slightest move in her direction or a hand up the back of her massive purple jumper. Coyle had gone out well-oiled towards the end of the night to confirm what you all knew. What you could all scent by the dock infested lawn, the barrow full of clippings brimming with pungent water, the silent three stories of Edwardian bay windows vinyl black and lifeless and unvexed by your presence. Empty. Bravado pushed him to it. And a nervous system overloaded with the crystal shudder of eight cans of lager. He built it up, searching the garden gone to seed for the right sized rock and the camp was split evenly between the conscientious ah for fucks sake man sit down and the anxious give it over Coyle you arsehole to the passive onlookers wanting the smash and whatever came after but not wanting to say. He was amped by the attention and when he had the stone in his fist and the lot of you looking out from the doorway of the glasshouse he had no option but to stride purposefully towards the back of the building which inhaled him into its cavernous black bay eyes and draped his approach with the sobering aeons of silence step that took him step to the precipice step of action step or inaction. Smash. And at the tittering chime you all ran, fighting through the shed door, haring for the bushes in a choked effulgence of strangled laughter, shouts and tangled hands on shoulders on smalls of backs on napes of necks of lips on the thin crest of ear of her reaching behind and finding your fingers and shearing off into the buddleias. And suddenly they were a continent away in mad tangles of rhododendrons fighting through the chainlink fence. Dark. Jet black giving way to the grainy pixelated greyness that cushioned yet somehow exaggerated sound. Breaths mostly. Hands found the perches of her hips and you bent to find the tongue that was waiting in her mouth full of voltage. Bestowed its electricity on you. And you gave back you don't know what, struggling with her rhythm, losing your breath, heavy nose breathing and bringing your hands in at her waist and following up her back sliding beneath the jumper feeling the apparatus of brazier beneath her t-shirt and up to her shoulders and palping the back of her neck and hoping to Christ this was ok and that she wasn't looking for more – or less and swelling when she responded slipping her arms inside your jacket and around your ribs. You emerged when the others came creeping back into the unexploded silence, drawn by the catgut line of curiosity through the chainlink fence and up the overgrown path and past the mildewed glasshouse to the shard fringed window frame exhaling wounded energy, exhaling a longing, exhaling the dust of a stifled past, of lives lived into the damp, moon-bright youth-buoyed night. Coyle despite his amped up trajectory had not aimed wild and smashed one of the stately bays but had gone for a small sash window that opened into a space beneath the back stairs. When you cleared out the frame and climbed in, Coyle deferred and you took the initiative brimming with recent events. The place was immaculate. Dry, empty and covered in a film of chalky dust that you knew was down to the comprehensive removal of marble mantle pieces, wrought iron fireplaces and period furniture. A noise out front. A thump of panic like a bird against a windscreen. Coyle's voice through the letterbox let me eee-iii-ynnn. You opened the front door and there he stood, with her, framed by the gothic shape of the overhanging trees. In the hall, the majesty of the staircase and the red and black square tiles laid on the diagonal. A heavy black rotary dial phone riveted to the wall – still working. The bare light bulbs hanging in their sockets – operational. The toilet flushing. Bare boards upstairs rooms over rooms of unspoilt space and you were all, even Coyle, in awe of the nobility of the place. Of the third floor up in the rafters with the lattice and plaster walls and the dormer windows out onto the roof and the doughty chimney breasts. When the moon had passed low and the frost set in and the beers run out, you all left by the front door, not before coming together in the hall, all 12 of you. Acknowledged paradise. And you gravely undertook, one and all to maintain the secret. To not abuse. To be respectful. To not spread the word, pollute, desecrate or damage.

Go now up the overgrown path. Past the pile of stagnant clippings weeping on the paving. Past the smashed glasshouse with the upended barrow jammed in the frame, through the yawning maw of the empty bay window into the rain splashed and beer can obliterated back room. Say alright to whatever lads are in, talking shit and drinking fast and flinging cans off the walls. Pass into the hall with the stereo pumping shite metal and empty cans and broken glass skittering across the tiles and some fuckhead kicking out the balustrade posts and the black phone in pieces against the foot of a wall scored with deep meaningless gashes. Push past the bodies on the stairs up to the bare boards of the bedroom with wax candles melting into the timber and a conclave sitting around a creep with long straggly hair holding court about this great weed he's rolling into a baggy joint and counting out mushrooms from a paper bag. See all of the lightbulbs smashed out and the bath full to the brim with detritus and the heavy porcelain toilet broken into big wet chunky shards. Up again to the top floor and Coyle is there in the raging dark, stereo blaring with his shirt off ramming a balustrade post through the lattice wall as goblins crawl into the night through the skylight howling over the reluctant suburb. Howling for the police to come which sure as fuck they will in the end and run a surge of sixty, half-dressed, tripping heretics through the brutalised shell of the building, cramming through the back window, down the overgrown path and over the uprooted chainlink fence like sand hoppers churning through heaped banks of bladderwrack and chief fuck among them with a purple woollen jumper tied over his naked shoulders and her smell on the fingers of one hand and not fucking one of us will ever vocalise the fact, put words to it, make it real with sound – that this was the house where Ben our Australian classmate would bring us in our dozens for tea and computer games during long lazy lunch breaks all through transition year as his ailing grandmother boiled the kettle or sent apologies and warm greeting down from her bed above. Not one word of it uttered. Not one evocation of his name to humanise the space. To spell what we had done.

Amber Duivenvoorden

Amber Duivenvoorden is a Maltese writer currently doing an MA in Creative Writing at Lancaster University. She is working on short stories which explore familial relationships. Her writing is dominated by Malta – the country's gender and socio-economic problems, the landscape, and the effects on the individual. Her major influences are Thomas Hardy, Alice Munro, Milan Kundera, Ken Kesey and Katherine Mansfield, as well as French short story writers such as Sartre and Colette.

The Prickly Pears

At five o'clock, a strawberry sunrise had started its mastery over the fields and walls and trees and it was then that Pawlu and his boy Eman arrived on a cart with their mule. The axle turned slowly, the spoked wheels with it, their wooden rims gnawing at the rock-strewn road. In the distance loomed the Mdina Cathedral; the Corinthian pilasters of the dome and belfries in command of its baroque skyline, the bastions and houses and tufts of shrubbery falling away beneath it. The man pulled backwards on his mule's reins and the wheels came to a halt. Then the boy reached into the back of the cart for two buckets and clasping them tightly under his arms, he got off and went to wait for his father by the prickly pears. The cacti clustered around the rubble walls, their rounded lobes climbing, one on top of the other, struggling for space, protruding from the stones' soil-filled gaps.

It took Pawlu slightly longer to get down; his legs were curved outwards like sickle blades and he relied on his right foot to steady himself while dragging the left one behind. It took him a while to get to the tree, he was out of breath by then and leaned on the wall for support. His hand, furrowed with red lines and calluses closed around the egg-shaped fruit and pulled it away from the plant's ear, releasing it into the bucket. This ritual went on until the two buckets were full, then they loaded them onto the cart and continued their journey.

After a while, the boy's eyelids started to droop and his little head came to rest against his father's shoulder. The man looked down at his son and smiled. Today they would all be together; his eldest son was expected home from abroad. They were all preparing for his arrival. He'd left his wife rubbing sourdough bread with tomatoes and olive oil in the kitchen. She'd bought a short-sleeved jacket with a peplum and a full skirt. It was much like the Queen's in Friday's paper. Before leaving Rosa had asked him to zip her up, just in case their son arrived home early, she didn't want him to see her in her everyday clothes.

"Wake up, we're nearly there."

The boy opened his eyes slowly, raising a hand over his face, shielding it from the sun. "Today I want to peel them with you Pa. Can I, can I?"

"Maybe, if you're quiet."

Mari was sitting on the front step, peeling potatoes; her pale skin looked vulnerable against the rough tubers, their rind thick with earth. The boy ran up to her and she pulled him under her arm, kissing him on his head. "Did you get it? The fruit?" she asked.

"Yes, yes I helped Pa."

"Good, good," she said. "I think you should go finish it, before he gets here."

The boy hurried into the kitchen; oak beams ran along the low ceiling and the grainy, uneven limestone walls beamed mustard yellow, their white cement lines like tear stains, streaking the stone blocks. The skinned bodies of two rabbits lay beside each other on the kitchen counter, ripples of fat spreading across the pink flesh. They were laid on their sides so that both the hind and forelegs stretched away from their bodies. The heads had been chopped off. His father always killed them in the same way; he'd hold the hind legs together with one hand and put the other around their necks.

Then he'd tighten his grip, pressing his thumb into the back of their necks, pushing the chin up, pulling down on their legs. They always struggled but his father was too strong, you'd hear a cracking sound and then they'd go limp in his hands.

On the table was the paper Eman had been sketching on all morning. He'd drawn two figures, one, much taller than the other, next to a square house. Both had triangle bodies and rectangle legs and arms. He'd given them smiles that curved upwards to the dotted eyes and a line nose. The rectangle legs and arms sprouted web hands and feet. Above their heads was a thick blue stripe which ran across the page. The only thing missing was the hair colour. He wasn't sure what his brother's was. Eman had tried to picture him, how he'd looked before he'd left, but he couldn't. He had a vague memory of being lifted into the air and carried on the shoulders of a man with long, dark hair. He'd seen photos of his brother and sister in a field holding canes and one of his brother cutting a birthday cake, but everyone's hair colour looked the same in photos. You couldn't tell.

Pawlu came into the kitchen carrying the buckets of fruit. He paused in the doorway, lowered them to the floor and sat on the chair closest to the boy. He put his face in his hands.

"Are you tired?" asked the boy.

"Yes."

"Do you remember the colour of Twanny's hair?"

"Of course I remember the colour of my son's hair." Pawlu was looking out the window, shaking his head, his eyes fixed on something outside. "Of course I remember."

"What was it?"

"It's brown, brown, like your mother's."

"Maybe it's different now."

"No, it's the same, it hasn't changed." His elbow was on the table now, his hand hidden in his hair. He had two lines on each side of his nose that ran so deep they made his mouth and chin look separate from the rest of the face, as though they were cowering in the shadow of his nose.

"I think he looks different now. Maybe he has a proper beard and one of those moustaches that curl at both ends and maybe he's tall, really tall; tall like you. Maybe you won't even recognize him."

The man said nothing. He just kept on staring. Then he stood up and moved towards the buckets.

"Want to help me peel the fruit?"

They went through the kitchen into the yard.

"First we need to soak them in water; otherwise the thorns will hurt your hands."

Flowerpots lined the yard's walls. Most of them were rimmed with soil, some were cracked in places. At the end of the line were two empty buckets. Eman took one of them and went over to the water tap. He put his hand over the valve's metal handle and loosened it. Then he watched the water spurt in a line and whorl in the bucket, felt it grow heavier and heavier until he tightened the handle and it died quickly.

Pawlu took a fruit in his hand and lowered it in the water. Then he lifted it up. "Look closely," he said. Holding the prickly pear firmly between his fingers he chopped off its top, then he turned its severed head upside down and cut the other end. Next he made a cut down the side of the fruit, end to end, put his thumb under its skin and pulled it off, revealing the soft red mesh of its flesh.

"Here, eat it." Pawlu said, handing it to the boy.

"Don't give him too much to eat, he won't eat later on." His mother had come into the yard.

Rosa went over to the washing line hanging from wall to wall and started taking off clothes and putting them on her arm. She felt sweat beginning to slide down her forehead, dampening her armpits, her dress. There was an intermittent pain at the back of her head, like someone was pulling at her hair, then releasing their grip and coming again. When the line was clear she turned to her son and husband. The boy was concentrating on cutting through the thick peel. Rosa watched the naked fruit roll into his hand as he tossed the rind onto a few newspaper pages. He took up another fruit quickly as though he'd been doing this for years. Her husband's head was bowed, his hands moving quickly, from fruit to fruit, the knife barely visible in his hand, hidden between thumb and index finger. There was soil under his nails.

"Don't take long. You need to wash before he comes. Both of you."

She disappeared inside, holding the bundle against her chest.

"Mari have you finished with the potatoes?" she called out.

"Nearly."

"Bring them here, I'll finish them myself. Go get ready."

Rosa went into the bedroom and set the clothes on the bed. She took up a finger to the back of her head and pressed where it hurt. If she pressed hard enough the pain stopped. She moved towards the dresser and sat on the stool and smiled. It had been such a long time. The last time she'd spoken to him, really spoken, he was so young, so ready to leave home, this small, small island he called it, there was nothing for him there and she knew it. And he was right, so right. What great success he'd had! How lucky he'd been. And now he would come back, nicely dressed, refined, like those men she saw walking down Archbishop Street when they went to Valletta. They always carried leather suitcases and walked fast, their eyes never quite meeting anyone else's on the street. At noon they'd come out of their offices, laughing and talking in high voices and eating in the café that used china teapots with violets on them. When Rosa saw them she always thought of him and how he too could be walking with his suitcase in a nice, black suit, laughing in a café surrounded with people like him.

She thought of the last time she'd seen him, standing in her kitchen, just before he'd left. She could still feel the softness in his flannel shirt, the sprouting of stubble along his jaw, hear his voice, the ring in it, like there was always something important to say, something urgent. Rosa often went over memories of him in her mind and there were many of them; him at the beach, helping his father with the animals, playing with his sister, however there was one that seemed stuck in her mind. It repeated itself like the same record playing in a gramophone over and over again; it was of him when he was much younger, her daughter hadn't been born then. They were sitting in a field and a ladybird had settled on his hand. He'd watched the insect traverse the length of his arm, then when it flew off, he'd looked about him, expecting to find it. He said he had to find it, it was going to be his new friend. She'd watched him searching in the cracks between the stones in the rubble walls, in the shrubs lining the walls, scattered across the field until he'd given up and come back to her, wrapping his arms around her shoulders, asking her to take him home for tea.

Rosa stood up to hang the clothes in the closet. Her daughter was standing in the doorway.

"Did you put the potatoes in the kitchen?" Rosa asked, taking up one of her husband's shirts.

"The telegram boy just brought this." Mari said holding out a piece of paper.

"What is it? What does it say?"

Mari opened the letter, then looked up at her mother.

"It's Twanny," she said. "He's not coming. Here."

Rosa took the letter from the girl. At first, all she saw were black dashes stretched out on a sheet. She blinked once, twice.

Sent you a letter which might arrive late. Can't come home this time. New job opportunity in San Francisco. Will write soon. Greetings.

Antoine Gatt.

There was silence for some time. The woman couldn't take her eyes off the paper, she read the lines again and again. Those three lines, some black dashes across a white sheet. Again and again. Then the paper slipped out of her hand and fell to the floor. She looked at her daughter, her hair tied up in a messy knot, her eyes wide, fixed on Rosa, then at the walls, the paint cracking in corners, at the clothes on the bed. She thought of the rabbits in the kitchen and the bread, of her husband and son, heads bowed at the fruit. The pain came again, sharp. She lifted the finger to her head and closed her eyes.

"Ma, we've finished the prickly pears, they're all done." The boy was tugging at her skirt. She opened her eyes. All she saw were two scribbled figures on a sheet.

"Do you like this colour for Twanny's hair? It's dark brown like yours."

Jennifer Harvey

Jennifer Harvey is a Scottish writer now living in Amsterdam. Her stories have been published in various magazines and anthologies in the US and the UK including: Bare *Fiction*, *The Lonely Crowd*, *Folio*, and *Carve*. She is a Resident Reader for *Carve Magazine* and loves discovering good stories in the 'slush pile'. When not writing, she can be found sauntering along the Amsterdam canals, dreaming up new stories.

ESO 378 Nebula

He tells her, 'There's a giant bubble floating way out in the darkness of space. A planetary nebula. Do you know what that is?'

She shakes her head, wonders how it is he knows so much already. It's not a trait he has inherited from her, this curiosity about obscure things, this strange, formal way of explaining them. The way a teacher would a pupil, or a parent a child. Only in their case the roles are reversed. It is he who explains to her the way things work.

'It's the remnants of a dying star,' he continues. 'It's not a bubble at all, really. It's just that sometimes the facts, and what is observable, collide.'

And he flicks through the book until he finds the right page then turns it round to show her.

ESO 378 Nebula,' he says. 'ESO, that means it was taken by the European Southern Observatory. The number, well, that's for identification. And nebula, that's the classification. It tells you what it is.'

The details are important, and she knows not to interrupt until he has told her everything. She knows to nod as each piece of information is delivered.

When he finishes, she looks at the photo and is surprised, because seen from earth, seen from some light-hearted moment, some childish point in time, it really does looks like a soapy bubble.

'The kind of bubble God would blow, if he were that way inclined,' she says.

And he laughs and turns the page towards him so he can look at it again, reappraise it, in light of this new, wholly unscientific statement.

'Yes,' he says, 'If I were God, I suppose this is the sort of bubble I would blow.'

Though she can see from his smile, from the gleam in his eyes that he is amused she sees things this way, so she throws his own words back at him, hoping he might explain them.

'Sometimes the facts and what is observable collide.'

But he doesn't look up from the book, just mutters, 'yup', then turns and walks away. She has lost him again to this world which lies beyond her. To things she struggles to understand.

'Nebulous,' she thinks, and she smiles. 'Yes, that's the word for it. For the way she feels.'

Two days after the bubble incident the phone rings. The school. Can she come down? They need to 'have a word.'

'Is everything okay?' she asks. 'With Edward. Is everything okay?'

If she could just 'come down,' they repeat.

She thinks about calling Adam but can't think what she would say to him.

'It's the school. They called again. About Edward.'

Again. They called again.

She can't keep bothering him with these things. Troubling him about their son.

If there's a problem she can tell him afterwards. And if there is none? What then?

Another little secret she and Edward can keep from him?

Well, why not? It won't be the last secret they keep.

Instead she thinks of all the reasons the school has had so far for calling her. All those telephone calls that begin the same.

'It's Edward, Mrs Moore. Can you come down?'

Each incident blurring into one. The snow globe, the butterfly, the matches, the apple.

'What will it be this time?' she wonders. Though a part of her can already imagine. ESO 378. Though how a cloud of gas and dust way out in space can lead to trouble in a classroom, she can't imagine. Though a piece of her is intrigued, a piece of her wants to find out.

But the bigger piece wants to run.

'It's Amy Peterson,' the teacher explains.

'Right, I see,' she sighs.

And the teacher tilts her head to the side, as if she's bemused. As if she's thinking, 'Oh, so you know about Amy?'

In fact, this is what she says.

'Oh, so you know about Amy?'

'I know that her mother died, yes. About a year ago, wasn't it?'

'Six months,' she corrects.

But already she is only half listening because she's trying to think of the connections. Amy's mother. A planetary nebula. Edward. How would he connect these things?

'She believes in heaven. Amy that is,' the teacher explains. 'And we let her talk about it, because it's a comfort to her, as I'm sure you can understand.'

And it's not that Edward wouldn't believe in heaven. He'd be open to the idea, she's sure of it. But he would want some sort of proof, some reasoning and explanation.

And she's about to tell this to the teacher but doesn't get a chance.

'Mrs Moore, as you know, there have been plenty of incidents this year and we've tried to accommodate your son.'

'Accommodate him,' she thinks. As if he's some sort of exception, a thing to be tolerated, a thing they need to find a special place for. And he is, of course.

'Accommodate?' she repeats.

'Yes,' the teacher continues. 'Make room for him, so he can express himself.'

'Listen,' she says, 'Can you please just tell me what happened. I don't need you to be polite. I know my son. I know he's not easy. Just tell me what he's done and tell me what's going to happen.'

'Right, yes. It can't be easy…'

'It's not. So, tell me.'

Though she already knows how the story goes. As soon as she heard the name, Amy, she had imagined it.

There'd be a conversation about heaven and its place in the universe, Edward explaining the existence of things, the known things, like nebula and stars and planets and moons. The continuous expansion, accelerating, perhaps towards heaven, but the journey incomplete, as yet, heaven just out of reach, always out of reach. Not really there at all, because it is always beyond.

'Nebulous' that word again. And she has said it out loud without meaning to and doesn't know how to explain.

'I'm sorry, what? Nebulous did you say?'

She ignores it and asks, 'did he tell her heaven doesn't exist? Is that what he said to her?'

'More or less,' the teacher tells her. 'He demanded proof, and when Amy could give him none she became upset, told him how terrible it was that he could be right. Perhaps heaven doesn't exist. And as you can imagine…'

She doesn't need the teacher to finish.

'Too much. Yes, that would be too much.'

'They're only ten,' the teacher says, though why she thinks to bring this up now is a mystery.

'Is this a conversation kids that age should not be having?' she wants to ask. 'Is there an age for such things?'

Though when she thinks of Edward, she can't quite imagine it, that he would put a limit on things.

'He's just a curious child is all,' she says. Again.

'In every sense of the word,' the teacher smiles.

And they agree to have him stay home a few days so he can 'think carefully about the way words too can cause unnecessary suffering.'

'Sometimes the facts and what is observable, collide,' she thinks as she gets up to leave. Though she keeps it to herself.

They drive home. In silence at first, because she has learned that quiet anger works best with him. It is something he understands.

But she cannot maintain the silence as long as he can.

'I heard Amy Peterson was upset.'

'Is that why I need to go home?'

'Surely you can understand that, Edward?'

'No,' he says. 'Explain it to me.'

And not for the first time she finds herself remembering those days when he was very small still and unable to talk. The easy peace of those days when all communication was conducted by touch and looks and soft, happy childish sounds, approximations of words that held no meaning beyond the comfort they provided. She remembers the soft down of his hair, how it stayed that way for almost two years, so that there was a babyish quality to him that was endearing and sweet.

'How did he go from that quiet easy child to this?' she wonders. Even though she knows it's not true. Because she remembers the intensity of his gaze, even when he had no words. It was as if he was talking. Observing things, weighing them up, commenting wordlessly. As if he had been considering the world for millennia.

Such a strange child.

And now she must explain it to him. Well, okay.

'You know what it means when someone dies, Edward, don't you?'

'Yes,' he says. 'They cease to exist.'

'And you know how that can hurt people? When someone they love dies.'

'Like that butterfly,' he says. Not a question but a statement. As if the death of one or the other was the same. And maybe it is, who is she to say?

'All Amy wanted, was to know her mum was safe, that's all.'

And he surprises her. 'Of course. I understand that.'

'You do?' and she wishes she had not sounded so surprised because he turns to look at her, and she has to slow the car down and focus on the road because the feeling there, at the side of her head as he stares at her is so strong. Like the grip of a vice.

'Then explain it to me,' she tells him.

And he does.

'Amy Peterson doesn't eat her lunch,' he begins. 'Every day she takes her sandwiches and when she thinks no one is looking, she empties the contents of her lunch box into the bin. And every day I see her do it. And so I told her. I told her: I see what you do with your lunch, Amy, and I really don't think that's the best way to get back to your mum.'

And she slows the car right down then and rolls into a lay-by and stops the car.

'You said that to her?'

'Yes,' he says.

'But why? What do you mean?'

'I just told you, she throws away her lunch. Every day.'

'Yes, I know. But what's that got to do with her mum?'

And he looks at her and frowns, a small crease which sits between his brows, more perplexed than anything else.

'She'll die. If she stops eating, then she'll die,' he says. 'Don't you think?'

She needs to take a moment. 'Breathe,' she thinks. Because Amy is such a bright child, like sunshine. Her happiness is not something anyone would consider fragile, even after all that has happened. And she wonders if perhaps Edward has made some sort of mistake.

'So, what did she say then?' she asks him. 'When you told her it was a bad idea.'

'She told me to leave her alone.'

'But you didn't.'

'Yes. I did. But only after I explained it to her, first. Why it is she can never get to heaven.'

'Right, I see. And why is that then, exactly?'

'No one can,' he tells her. 'No one.'

'You sound so certain of it. Surely an unknown can't contain so much certainty?'

'Yeah, I know that. But I don't think Amy does. So, I asked her. I said: tell me where it is then. Heaven. And she couldn't of course. And I said that that was okay, because it was always out of reach. That this was the reason the universe was expanding, faster and faster; so that however close we got, we would never be able to get there. It will always be out of reach. The only way to get there is to be allowed in. And, of course, if you don't eat your sandwiches, if you do something like that, well, I really don't think they would allow you in, do you? '

And the quality of this statement, the vagueness of it, spiritual, metaphysical and so matter of fact, makes her laugh. Coming from anyone else, she would simply nod and utter a polite 'yes'. But from Edward, it seems comical and unexpected and beyond even his seemingly limitless precociousness.

'She believed me though,' he continues. 'So I think, from now on, she"ll eat her lunch. Which is a good thing.'

And she wants to turn the car around and head back to school, confront the teacher with this new information, let her see that her son is not some strange creature, some difficult, unwieldy child. That he is observant, kind, intelligent. That he knows it can take a lie sometimes, to set someone straight.

And, as if he reads her thoughts he laughs and says, 'Don't. Let's just go home, enjoy a few days away from that place.'

As she shifts the car into gear she sneaks a look at him. His head rests against the window and he stares into the hedgerow as if he's asleep with his eyes closed.

'Edward,' she begins, but she gets no further, just squeezes the accelerator and pulls back out onto the road.

Because she has nothing to say and neither does he. They understand one another again, the way they did when he was that wordless, speechless child. And she's surprised at how comforting it feels. If she was to push the accelerator too hard now, speed down the road until they came to a juddering halt against some tree. If it were to end now, like that, it would be okay.

Adam comes home to find them in the kitchen pouring over an encyclopaedia, engrossed in the information it contains. All the wonders of the universe are laid out there, or that's how it seems to her.

'Gee, is that the time already?' she says when she sees Adam walk in. 'We've been side-tracked by all these stars.'

And Edward lifts up the book so his father can see it and says something about red dwarves, but Adam doesn't listen. Just nods a perfunctory 'sounds pretty cool,' then heads to the fridge and fetches them both a beer.

'I'll order something in, yeah?' she asks.

'Pizza!' Edward's immediate response. His response a relief, hinting as it does at something she tries not to long for. Something carefree.

It's only then Adam focuses in on them, and the chaotic spread of materials on the table – paper, pens, rulers, tin foil, scribbled notes and diagrams.

'Looks like you've been busy quite a while,' he says.

And before she can stop him Edward explains, 'the whole day almost. There's so much to find out.'

Adam shoots her a look but says nothing, just takes a sip of his beer and lifts up one of the drawings Edward has made.

'That's a nebula,' he tells his father.

Adam stares at the drawing and turns it around examining it from various angles.

'Did something happen at school?' he finally asks.

'I'll order the pizza,' she says. 'We can talk about it later. Mushroom okay?'

And she looks at Adam as he stares at his son. If he could pick him up and turn him around, examine him from every angle, inside and out, she knows he would. But it's not fascination she sees in his face. It's not even frustration. Rather, it's something closer to resignation as if he's finally decided his son is beyond understanding now, and that, somehow, it's okay to simply give up.

And should she fight it, she wonders, or envy him that he has reached this stage?

They argue of course. When they have closed the door on Edward and he is asleep. When they know he cannot hear them.

With every incident Adam knows his case for intervention becomes stronger. But she is still prepared to resist. Thinks even, with every passing problem, that she will always resist. Because this is what she is meant to do. She expects it of herself and she knows Edward does too, though they have never spoken of it.

She told Adam everything just the same. About Amy, heaven, the nebula. And he had listened silently, his gaze falling on a place somewhere beyond her, as if he was unable to look at her directly. But she thought perhaps she saw a small flicker of something. A realisation and understanding that what she was telling him was more interesting than strange. It showed Edward was not what he appeared – not an awkward child, a special child. Simply the thoughtful child she had always understood him to be.

Though if she were honest, she would admit she has not always felt this way. And she remembers again the strangeness of his gaze as a baby, and how unsettled it had made her feel. There were many times she recoiled from her infant son, something which had shocked Adam. 'Cold hearted' the accusation he had thrown. A barb which had lodged deep within her, but which she had not been strong enough to challenge. Was not even sure if she should, because there was a chill there inside of her. It was true. The warming up took years.

But it arrived, and it has brought with it a strengthened will on her part to defend Edward after every incident, every argument.

'He should see someone,' Adam tells her. 'I don't know why you think he can go on like this. These exclusions from school, the solitariness – I mean, have you ever known a child with no friends? I mean, not a single one? How can that not worry you?'

'He's self-contained is all.' she says.

'Oh come on, Sarah! Don't give me that! No one likes him! He's weird. He needs help.'

The words filling the room before they notice Edward standing there, his head tilted, his eyes fixed on his father.

'They're not so likeable is all it is,' he says. Matter of fact, so they have no way of telling if he is hurt or offended or how much he has heard.

'Edward,' she says.

'Mum,' he replies.

And Adam simply stares and says nothing.

So she waits. Waits for Edward to indicate just how this is all going to pan out.

Waits for her ten year old son to calm the thudding in her chest.

'Ed,' Adam begins. 'Ed, I'm sorry.'

'Why?' Edward asks, and she can't be sure he is unaware of the threat this one word contains. The challenge it poses.

'You meant it,' he continues. 'So why be sorry?'

'Ed,' Adam pleads. 'I just want you to be happy is all.'

'I am happy,' he tells him. 'I am very happy.'

Then he turns and heads back to his room because nothing more needs to be said.

They will never speak of this incident, any of them. She knows that from the silence which fills the room., both of them staring at the empty doorway where Edward had stood.

She knows it from the silence which follows for days afterwards – 'this will last for weeks, months. Forever,' she thinks.

It is a distance which can never be breached. And she remembers the terrible blackness she had focussed on in those photos in the encyclopaedia. The emptiness of the universe. The distance between objects. And she wonders if she can believe it, that it's actually this distance which holds it altogether.

The school calls. Though this time they don't ask her to come down.

'I spoke to Amy today,' the teacher says.

'Oh. Is she okay?'

'Yes, yes she's fine. I just wanted to apologise.'

'Apologise?'   .

'Yes. I spoke to her some more about Edward. '

'Oh. What did she say?'

'She said he was perceptive. That he had a lot of thoughts going round in his head. But that he was right. About her that is'

'The lunch you mean?'

'He told you about that?'

'He tells me most things.'

'Right. Well, I'm glad he was looking out for her. It's very considerate of him. And I just wanted to say that we're all hoping Edward will return soon.'

And she wants to mention she had known this all along, but she lets it slide, lets the teacher have her moment. Accepts the apology for what it is – a vindication she is not allowed to acknowledge. She ignores the request to discuss his return. 'Let them wait,' she thinks.'

'Thanks for calling,' is all she says, then hangs up. Until the next call, which will come, of course it will come.

And she laughs at that. A big, out loud laugh that lasts so long she thinks she may fill the whole day with it. But when it ends, the worry begins again.

'Was that the school?' Edward asks her.

'Yes,' she tells him. 'They're wondering when you're coming back.'

'Oh,' he says. 'Am I? Am I going back?'

And she shrugs and says, 'only when you want to.'

And she's about to ask him when that may be. But he is gone. Just like that. Off to the corner of the room where a pile of papers lie scattered on the floor amongst a heap of tools and objects, some of which she can't identify.

The nebula is gone. The universe. The mystery of all that. Replaced by more prosaic things. First stones unearthed in the garden. Then bark peeled from the birch. And now wood, it would appear, which he is cutting to size to form something only he seems to understand. Every day brings a new project, a new investigation. Things studied with an intensity she would find too ferocious, too peculiar, were it not for the fact she has simply grown used to it.

And sometimes she imagines it, the way these things must fire inside him, the ideas shooting through his brain and exploding somewhere. Somewhere deep within the folds of tissue and glowing nerves.

A universe within a universe, expanding and contracting. And if there is a purpose to it, nobody knows.

Though perhaps, she thinks, perhaps that is the point.

Conor Houghton

Conor Houghton is a computer scientist and neuroscientist who is concerned with mathematical ideas related to how the brain works. He grew up in the west of Ireland but now lives in the south west of England. His fiction has appeared in several publications including the 2017 National Flash Fiction Day Anthology and Bare Fiction Magazine. In 2016 he won the Doolin Literary Festival Flash Fiction Competition.

Big Secrets Everybody Knows

The space shuttle started flying in April 1981, the same time as the hunger strikes. I was nine back then and I used to play at space shuttle with my friend Síle. There was an old boiler in the field behind our house, it must have come from a factory but with the rust and huge round-headed bolts it looked like a part discarded from a ship. It was pyramid shaped with an opening, to us a doorway, in one side and a short thick pipe on top. Sitting inside looking up you could see a little disc of sky through the pipe, framed as through a telescope. Someone had painted an Irish flag and "IRA" on the outside; Síle used to steal stubs of chalk from school so we could write "NASA" on it as well, though the rain used to wash the chalk off from one day to the next.

One Saturday after lunch we were about to get into our space shuttle when we heard crying. We poked our heads in the door and found an adult sat inside all folded up to fit; knees by her face, like when I hid my rag doll in my lunch box to sneak her into school. I didn't know who the lady was, but Síle did. She whispered that she was Mrs McDaid from the other side of the village, whose husband Mr McDaid and dog Captain McDaid we knew and liked. We sometimes watched while Mr McDaid threw stones for Captain to chase into the sea. Síle said "My mam and dad were talking about how Mrs McDaid is carrying on with dad's friend Mr

Wherity. They said it's a big secret everybody knows."

I blessed myself because I was scared of the Wherity's dog, an Alsatian called Toby Wherity. Mrs Wherity was great friends with my mother and I'd often wondered how it was that my mother and Mrs Wherity were friends and Mr Wherity was friends with Síle's father even though my parents and Síle's parents weren't friends at all.

After a few minutes Mrs McDaid clambered out. She wasn't crying any more but her face was red and there were marks on her cardigan from the rust. We stood watching her and when she straightened herself upright I said "Hello Mrs McDaid" as politely as I could. "Do you know me?" she asked and I told her I did but that it was a big secret why. She asked what the secret was and I didn't know what to say. I didn't understand why Mrs McDaid was in our space shuttle but didn't want to ask in case it was normal. Síle said her father had told her mother that he couldn't explain what was happening "because Mrs Wherity is as cute as a bag of weasels".

At that Mrs McDaid started crying again, pushing her hands into her face like she'd gotten juice in her eyes. To cheer her up I told her that her dog Captain was nicer than Toby Wherity; she looked at me and said "I amn't really a bad person." I didn't know how to respond, we weren't used to thinking of adults as good or bad, except maybe the British. Mrs McDaid didn't say anything more so we smiled at her and got into our boiler.

That evening I discovered another big secret. Like most Saturdays we went to John Murphy's after tea so my father could have his pint. My parents sat as usual with Garda Healy and Mrs Healy while I sat with the other children at the space invaders table. Before Garda Healy was even halfway through his pint Mr Wherity came over and whispered something to him and all of a sudden the Healys all up and left, Garda Healy's half drunk pint was abandoned on the table with its rings of froth.

A couple of minutes later Joe Joe Kavanagh came in with a scarf on his face and a black beret on his head. He was wearing sunglasses even though it was the evening and anyway we were inside. He walked around collecting money in a bucket and giving out little Irish-flag ribbons on pins. Everyone must have known it was Joe Joe but they all pretended they didn't; like it was a secret. He looked over at our table and my mother reached for her purse but my father put his hand on her arm to stop her.

I wondered if Joe Joe had left his dog Shep outside. Shep Kavanagh was one of those black and white collies and wasn't the sort of dog you could talk to, but I liked watching her help Joe Joe herding cows up the Letterkenny Road for milking.

Later I asked my brother what the big secret about Joe Joe was and he said "do you mean what him and Síle's dad and Mr Wherity do up in the Up The Hill Woods?". I didn't want to seem ignorant so I nodded yes. I asked Síle about it when I saw her and she said she didn't know. We almost had an argument because I thought she knew more than she was telling and I didn't like to think of her keeping secrets from me.

After lunch on Sunday Síle and I set off for the Up The Hill Woods. I hadn't wanted to go because of Síle keeping secrets and because the woods were a good way the other side of the Letterkenny Road, which we were forbidden to cross, but Síle couldn't be stopped and I didn't want to be left out. When we got there, the woods were full of wild garlic and I was a bit scared tramping through it with the leaves and flowers brushing my legs. I liked the smell though, it made me think of the summer coming.

We weren't walking long when we came to the clearing; beautiful like one of the places where witches live in books. It was wide enough that the sun lit up some of it in patches but other bits were lit in dapples from the sun shining through the leaves. The clearing was much longer than it was wide, like it was for running short races. The grass was a thousand colours, all green. I heard a grasshopper singing in the grass and tried to find it, I liked the machine look of their legs and I liked the tingly feeling you got inside if you caught one and it moved in your cupped hands. I couldn't see the grasshopper but I found a bullet casing, bigger than the shells from the rifle my dad had for shooting rabbits.

Síle seemed a bit worried about the shell, she told me not to tell her father about it, as if I would. I loved it though, so shiny. As we walked home I held it with my thumb over the hole and imagined it contained a genii who I could force with a wish to explain all the secrets I didn't understand.

On the Wednesday of that week we had a half day because our teacher had a funeral to go to. We walked over to the McDaid's house, not to the front, we went the back way through the old cement factory. They had a bungalow with a kennel for Captain and a big vegetable patch in the back garden all neatly dug over in ridges. The house seemed empty but we peaked into the windows one-by-one and in the back bedroom we saw Mrs McDaid lying on the bed. Mr Wherity was there and as we watched he stuck his head under her dress. It looked like she was letting him look at what we called her wee wee, like we'd heard Mary Ann from the class above us had done with Garda Healy's boy. I found it a bit frightening, but Síle wanted to stay.

Just then we heard a car out front; Mrs McDaid must've heard it too and she said something to Mr Wherity. We found it a funny sight seeing him try to get out from under her dress, her legs and his head all tangled. We were still laughing when Mr Wherity came out the back door and saw us. Síle said "Hello Mr Wherity" in a nice clear voice and I was glad she was so brave because Mr Wherity looked very angry. Mr Wherity put his finger to his lips to mean "shush" and went down on hunkers beside us by the window. He said "whatever you saw is a big secret, don't tell anyone or there'll be trouble, Síle you know I'm not a man to mess with."

Next thing Mrs McDaid came back into the bedroom but now with Mr McDaid and they were kissing. We watched, all three of us; Mr Wherity kneeling and the two of us each side of him, like a picture of a praying saint being visited by little angels. Soon they were lying on the bed, still kissing, and Mrs McDaid pushed Mr McDaid away a bit and said something and it looked like Mr McDaid was going to stick his head under her dress like Mr Wherity had. Mr Wherity whispered "you better go now girls and remember what I said."

As we were climbing the fence we looked back and Mr Wherity was still kneeling there watching through the window. His back was to us, but it looked like he was fiddling with his fly, Síle said she thought he was going to wee against the wall of the house but I wasn't sure since it would've gotten all over the knees of his trousers.

That evening before bedtime we were allowed out for an hour and so we went down to the rocky shore. As we hoped, Mr McDaid was there with Captain, throwing stones into the sea. Captain would rush in each time like he expected to find the stone in the water. We collected some flat stones and tried skimming them and Mr McDaid asked to have a go. He was in great form and really good at skimming, sometimes he'd throw a sixer or sevener, leaving a trail of little circles that looked just for a second like the circles in a comic when someone is thinking.

The next day, when I got home from school, Mrs Wherity was in our kitchen having tea and biscuits with my mother. They went quiet as I came in and Mrs Wherity looked like she'd been crying. I thought maybe there was another secret to learn so I asked what they were talking about. It seemed I was right because my mother said "oh a big secret not for little ears" and to show off I said "is it like the big secret everyone knows about

Mr Wherity carrying on with Mrs McDaid."

There was a clatter as Mrs Wherity dropped her mug and spilled her tea and a big fuss cleaning it up and Mrs Wherity saying sorry again and again and then all of a sudden she was saying "bye" and was gone. My mother said to me "why did you go and say that" and I said I didn't know it was wrong, though I did a bit. I asked did Mrs Wherity not know the big secret. My mother said she did but that maybe she didn't know it was a "big secret everybody knows." She asked me what "carrying on" meant. I said it was "showing your wee wee to someone" and my mother laughed and told me not to be silly and she said she hoped I wasn't showing my wee wee to anyone.

Two days later was Saturday and we were in John Murphy's again. Mr Wherity was sat at the bar on his own with no sign of Mrs Wherity. I was just asking my dad for money for a blue Snack bar when Mr McDaid came bursting in, pushing the door so hard it made things shake on the shelf where the old trophies were. He made as if to box Mr Wherity. Garda Healy jumped to his feet and grabbed his arm to hold him back. The whole pub was in commotion.

Mr Wherity looked at Mr McDaid and said "Ah now John you know you can't do anything to me." Mr McDaid started shouting.

He said "I don't care if you're a hard man and your friends are hard men and I don't care if you're fighting your stupid war for Ireland, or if you build bombs in your garage or bury guns in your field; you and your fucking secrets, your secrets have done more harm to Ireland than the British ever have. It's secrets that let the priests and politicians and every sort of gombeen bollocks do what the fuck they like here. It's secrets that wreck everything here and it's secrets that've let you wreck my family. They aren't even proper secrets, every fucker except me knew. Secrets aren't secrets, secret is just a name we give things so that we don't have to do anything about them."

I realized that Joe Joe and Síle's dad had come in quietly and were standing by the door watching. Joe Joe wasn't wearing his disguise but he was standing like he did when he had the scarf on his face, straighter, squarer. Síle's dad said to Mr McDaid "come on out with us John." His voice was different too, lower and louder at the same time. Garda Healy started to say something but Síle's dad said "leave it" and Garda Healy let go of Mr McDaid. Mr McDaid looked scared but determined at the same time, like a boy at the dentist's after he's told to be big and brave.

The next Tuesday Bobby Sands died and my teacher cried at school. There were black flags along the shopping street and everyone was very serious, men were stood at corners smoking and talking. I laughed watching Mr McDaid trying to throw stones for Captain while balancing on his new crutches; even better he let me throw some stones when I asked. My father told me not to make a big fuss about it but not to go around to Síle's house for a while. I didn't mind, I'd had a fight with Síle because she wouldn't explain any of the big secret about her dad and Joe Joe and what happened with Mr McDaid. It made me sad we weren't friends any more and it made me lonely to play space shuttle on my own, but I decided it was just like what Mr McDaid said about secrets ruining things. That made me feel very grown up.

Stephanie Hutton

Stephanie Hutton is a writer and clinical psychologist based in Staffordshire. She has had several pieces of work published online and in print. She gained second prize in the National Flash Fiction Day Micro Competition, and has been shortlisted in several competitions including the Black Pear Press Short Story Competition and The Brighton Prize. She has been selected for the Writing West Midlands Room 204 Writer Development Programme for emerging writers. She co-runs a community project, The Writing Kiln, and has initiated the regional Potteries Prize. Her work is available at stephaniehutton.com.

Born from Red

The school is on lock-down for a random colour check and I hear whispers that Leila has climbed out of the bathroom window, taking her painted toenails to safety. The rule is absolute; we must not see red. We line up in rows of cream and grey with our shirt sleeves rolled up. Our skirts touch our knees, showing pimply flesh where the hairs have been waxed as we are not permitted blades. Any scratch or cut must be covered with a bandage. It is safer to stay at home until your body is back the way it is intended – without the colour of the devil.

I have heard there is a nurse who checks that all girls are taking their medication – no menstruation is allowed of course as that is the fiercest red there is. There was a girl in the year above me who had vomited out her meds, or forgotten them, or had a dark desire to see her own blood. She was dismissed that day. We had to hang our heads and stare at the floor as she was escorted out. I wriggled my toes to wave goodbye but the rigid leather of my shoes hid my cowardly act.

After the checks, there is a shared relief that shows itself in skittishness and rumours. It is the one afternoon of the term when the instructors – all male of course – lean back in their chairs and permit whispers between us. I wonder at their intentions. The best way to keep control is to let our mouths spread stories and blame. My classmates' tongues click away at her name – Leila, Leila, Leila. I sit straight-backed and count with each breath to tame my heartbeats. Even as I recite poetry in my head, I see the image of my blood red heart beating her name, sending the urge to run down into my legs. I am grateful that it is Friday and I have two days of freedom to find her. She will not return to class on Monday.

Once the sun is high up above us, I tell dad I have botany specimens to collect and will be back by supper time. He is gluing small parts onto a ship that looks no different to any of the others he has made. He glances up from his handiwork to me and – although I squeezed my hands into a fist in preparation – I can't help but look away from the scarlet filaments that streak his eyes. These rivulets of red tell a story of lonely nights with only a vodka bottle to hold. My mother chose not to move to the safety of this village before I even started school. We do not speak of her. I hear the pulsing blood in my ears that keeps me alive while threatening to ruin me.

'No sharps, stay clean Anna,' he says and wraps some bread in cloth for me to take. I hold my breath as I kiss the top of his head, as if to stop him inhaling my intentions.

I take the path that leads from the back of our row of cottages towards the woods. The bluebells that kissed these grounds have already gone for another year. I walk fast enough to ache the back of my legs and burn my chest. Stillness or speed, nothing in-between. The curves of the path are as familiar as those of my signature. I once tried to walk the length with my eyes closed, certain that I could navigate the route. The elation of the first twenty yards was smashed as I tripped over and landed on my hands. Criss-cross lines in the forbidden colour kept me off school for a week and caused me such shame I stayed in bed with the drapes drawn to dull the hue.

I settle by the stream on a welcoming bank of grass to wait for her. This is our spot. She showed me how to fish with just a stick and fast hands.

Leila wears no sun cream or hat so her skin is older than her years, brown and rich. I am slathered in lotion to ensure that no patches of red appear on my shoulder blades or across my nose. We are taught that lips are naturally pink, but Leila's are as red as they are plump. She laughed when I told her this, curling my hair behind my ear. She told me of food from her grandmother's farm hidden high in the hills. The luscious tomatoes and sweet dripping apples, the opposite of green.

I doze in the warmth, the sunlight drifting through the mesh of my hat.

Leila speaks my name and tickles the back of my hand with a fern. My words won't come. She flings off her shoes and wobbles on one foot to show me her toenails. The rumours were true – they are painted a red so shiny I squint.

'I've got something for us to try, if you like.' Leila talks through her hands, which curl around each word and continue talking after her mouth stops. Sometimes they talk instead of her lips, like the time she pulled me to the roadside to look at the crushed bloodied carcass of a deer. She uncurls her hand and shows me little red and white mushrooms. I clench my teeth. Then nod.

We climb a little further into the trees for cover. Leila doesn't get out of breath like I do. She knows facts that are not in any book that we are allowed. I don't ask her how she knows. She tells me that these are toadstools, like in the fairy tales. I recall them being dusky pink and pure white. Leila laughs with her head tipped back, the length of her neck on view.

'Listen Anna, you don't have to take them with me. They could make us pretty sick. But before they do, they will show us a different world.' She is glowing. I tell myself that my nausea is excitement. My last weekend with Leila. I catch myself digging my nails into my palms and stop before any marks are made.

Leila arranges the toadstools on a piece of bark and chops them with a knife she pulls from her pocket. I long to run my finger along its edge. We chew the foamy pieces and sip river water from a flask, then we share my bread. Leila tells me she is going to go and work on her grandmother's farm, just outside the limits of the village. They keep animals I have never been near. My head starts to whirl as she tells me about lambs getting stuck in their mothers and pigs that reject their young. She has not just learnt this from letters sneaked in through the delivery boy – she must have been out there, in the world we were born into. The elbow I'm leaning on collapses under me, so I lie flat on the grass hearing the thud of the land. Leila's legs shake until she drops down to the ground near me and lies down. I feel the sting of bile at the back of my throat.

'Don't fight it Anna, let it show you things. I'm right here.'

She grabs my hand and the trees bend towards me as if to hold us together. I can't tell if it is the trees spinning around and around or us. Or have we only just noticed that the world is turning? I laugh and she sings. The grass underneath my body shoots up around us and springs into flowers larger than my head. Ripples run up and down my body as if I am at the lying on the riverbed.

I float up above the forest floor, higher and higher. Our village of green fields, pink flowers and white houses. There is the school, glowing so brightly I squeeze my eyes for protection. Then I dive down, down towards the ground, which opens beneath me. I land in a labyrinth of tunnels and press my back against hot earthy walls. Rivers of red run under the school, flowing outwards to escape to the forest. Swimming in the claret waters are beautiful women with their swollen pregnant forms. They turn to float on their backs, smiling and singing to their unborn. Standing waist-high in the lapping water, a couple intertwine while kissing – their hands grip and swirl across each other. I look more closely at the liquid. In the place of disgust, I feel peace and passion and what it is to be a woman. We were all born from red.

My body rises and floats easily out of the tunnels as my eyes linger on the scene I wish to stay in. Everything turns pure white as I return to my breathing body. The lulling waves change to stormy seas and I turn to my side to retch again and again. Sweat pours from the back of my neck as I free my stomach of all its bitterness.

My limbs start to obey my commands. The trees are back in their place, nothing but tall conifers swaying in the wind, oblivious to us. I turn to Leila and smile. She squeezes my hand in hers. Then I remember. My mother's hand encasing mine as she sang sweet melodies. My father screaming that her summer dress showed her off like a whore. The smash of his bottle. Red flowing down her arm. A pool of blood with shards of glass between us. Her shouting at me to keep away, to go to my room and stay under the covers. And later, again and again, dad on his knees, rocking forward and back as he prayed. Mumbling words through liquor-warmed lips, begging the Lord to keep us safe from the devil that lives in all women.

The danger is not out there, beyond the pastel safety of our village limits. It is not inside me. It is not a colour. I stand up and scan the higher land beyond the fencing. Paths curve their way up through the sloping fields – invitations in a thousand directions. One of them leads to my mother.

Leila still holds my hand as we make our way along an overgrown path towards the outskirts of the village. Our embracing fingers do the work of words. As the sun sets, the pink and white of the sky merge at the horizon into a deep red.

Kate L Jefford

Originally from Cardiff, Kate L. Jefford lives in London & Folkestone. She works in NHS & Student Mental Health services and is completing an MA in Creative Writing at Birkbeck. She won 1st prize in the H G Wells Short Story competition (2013) & 3rd prize in the Sunderland-Waterstones Short Story competition (2016). She has also been shortlisted in a number of writing competitions, including Bare Fiction & Fish Short Story Prizes. Her work is published in various print anthologies and MIR online. She's working on her first novel with support from lots of people who know who they are.

They Even Painted Over Dead Flies

They Even Painted Over Dead Flies

'Listen to me,' their mother used to say. 'I'm your mother.'

For as long as they can remember Di and Owen called her Muth.

Muth told them their father died. In an accident.

Muth was allocated a council a house on the new estate. There was a black line around the downstairs walls from when the river at the end of the street broke its banks. Before they moved in, the council re-decorated.

'They even painted over dead flies,' Muth said.

A Man-shaped Shadow

Di used to have a recurring dream: thunder crashing, lightning cracking, rain lashing the windows. She's crouched behind the settee with Owen, Muth's arms around them, Di hears another sort of racket, sees a man-shaped shadow through the frosted-glass panel in the front door.

'God's moving the furniture in Heaven and naughty Jesus is flicking the lights on and off,' Muth says. 'Nothing to be scared of.'

Only Di knows there's a man bashing the door with his fists.

Years later she described this dream to Muth.

'That wasn't a dream,' said Muth.

They Didn't Say Expelled But That's What It Was
Muth unpicked old jumpers to make crinkly balls of wool and knitted cardigans for them. She bought a second-hand typewriter, taught herself. *The quick brown fox jumps over the lazy dog.* Di used to listen to her practise. Clack. Click. Clack. Clack. Clack. In a few weeks it was clicketyclackclackclicketyclackclackclick. Ding. Zap.

With Di at school and Owen at nursery, Muth got a little office job. Until Owen stabbed another boy in the cheek with a pencil.

'It could've been his eye,' the teacher said.

Owen said the boy wouldn't let him lick his bubble-gum flavoured rubber. The teacher said the boy's father had given it to him. And asked Muth not to bring Owen back.

'They didn't say expelled but that's what it was,' Muth said.

Fathers for Justice
A photograph of Di and Owen aged six and five: Di in a Bo-Peep costume Muth made from an old petticoat of pale-blue nylon with a trim of pink roses. (No one'd know it wasn't satin.) Di's posed, holding the crook out on a straight arm. Her eyes are slits because she's facing the sun. Next to her, on all fours with a mop on his head and a white knobbly-knit jumper borrowed from Mr. Sale next door, Owen: forcing the smile Muth has instructed, cheeks blotchy and shining from tears.

Muth said she couldn't understand why Owen wanted to be Bo-Peep.

Di felt sorry for boys. If she wanted to pull on shorts or trousers, play football or climb trees, she could. She could also wear knee-high white socks and black patent-leather T-bars. She hadn't worked out what men were for.

Years later, after she'd qualified as a psychiatrist, Di would see a patient, a divorcee in a custody battle, a member of Fathers for Justice. He will see her once and make a complaint. He'll say he found some things she said, and her tone, hostile, indicating, he'll say, an issue with fathers of which she appeared unaware. Invited to respond to the complaint, Di won't be able to remember what she said. But she'll know he has a point.

Weston-super-Mare, 1968

Muth kept loose black-and-white photographs in an old Family Circle biscuit tin. Di's favourite was a photo of two young women on a beach, one fair, the other dark, one-piece bathing costumes taut over their pert, curvy curves. The fair one's Muth: head tilted, laughing, eyes shining. A look Di had never seen on her face. Scribbled on the back: *Weston-super-Mare, 1968.*

Once, Di came across a picture of a man, tall and wide as a wardrobe. Dark, not smiling, not even looking at the camera. She felt him tugging at something inside her, like fingers grabbing at her heart.

'Show me,' Muth said, when Di asked about him.

Di searched and searched. But the picture was gone.

Tears of Loss

Di used to wet the bed. She can't remember when it started but it was still happening in junior school. Days she woke up wet she'd walk to school feeling sick, and heavy like she'd swallowed stones, Owen skipping lightly at her side. She'd hold his hand, squeeze hard until he said, 'Ow'. Only then would she loosen her grip.

Muth tried everything to make the wetting stop. Slapping. Banning liquids before bed-time. Plonking her on the toilet in the night and running the tap. Giving her a talking to. Taking her to the doctor to get him to give her a talking to. None of it worked.

Di never picked the weeds they called 'wet-the-beds' so she'd no idea why it happened. Or why it was only her. Never Owen.

One morning, after Owen clunked downstairs, she slipped into his room, pulled her knickers down and peed on his bed. When they got home from school Muth's face told Di she knew before she felt the sharp burn of her hand on her legs.

Years later her therapist would say bed-wetting is crying, 'Tears of loss.'

'What loss?' Di would say.

She Must've Done Something To Deserve It

After she had the kids Muth suffered twinges in her lower back. She put it down to when her older brothers used to tie her in a chair with her skipping rope, and she'd wriggle and wriggle, twisting herself around. Her mother always said she must've done something to deserve it.

Some mornings the pain felt like an invasion of toxic insects. She pictured beetles in a frenzied state, pulsing and throbbing away inside her spine. Sometimes the pain reached her neck. It was all she could do not to shout. Sometimes she did. At the kids. She couldn't help it.

Tongues

Di and Owen practiced kissing like in films. In the airing cupboard where it was warm, dark, and they could hear Muth if she came upstairs. Just them, the tank wrapped in shiny red lagging, and Muth's bras draped from the hot-water pipes like Spanish Moss.

When Di had her first proper kiss she discovered they'd been doing it wrong, keeping mouths closed, lips shut. They hadn't known about tongues. Slobbery, slippy-slidey, writhing tongues. The boy nearly slurped her face off. She imagined all her insides sucked up through her gullet into his mouth.

Like Jam

Di and Owen weren't allowed up the far end of their street because:

1. The river could drown them and they would never be found because it was filthy and rat-infested and their bodies would end up far out to sea so they couldn't have a proper burial.

2. The cars could run them over because Muth said it was a rat-run and everyone was going too fast and they'd end up spread like jam on the road and the lids on their coffins would have to be closed.

3. The Johnsons lived up there.

Gate-Girl

End houses were for the biggest families because of the fourth bedroom and the garden like a fat wedge of pie on the corner.

As they approached the Johnsons' house, Di heard a noise like chalk on a blackboard and there, swinging on the Johnson gate, a girl about Di's age, bum stuck out, biscuit in her chubby hand.

'It's rude to stare,' the gate-girl said.

Di's legs locked. She couldn't stop staring. At the gate-girl's fat, creased arms, pink-rimmed eyes, pushed-up nose, and her hair! A crown of ringlets like a bunch of carrots.

'Miss Piggy! Miss Piggy! Nah-nah-nah-nah-nah,' Owen squealed, jumping up and down, pointing.

In a flash she was off the gate, lunging.

'Owwww,' Owen's hand shot to his cheek.

The girl ran inside, gate banging behind her, the biscuit, chocolate sucked off, on the pavement. Owen's eyes spilled. Silently. A lump of bloody skin hung off his cheek. Di took his hand. Very gently. They told Muth he fell. Guilt sloshed about inside Di. She vowed to protect her brother for ever and ever.

The World Doesn't Revolve Around You
Muth said:

Never swallow chewing gum, it will spin round your heart forever.

Never hit/kick each other or your hand/foot will stick up the grave.

It's like Piccadilly Circus/the Blackpool Illuminations/an oven in here.

The world doesn't revolve around you.

You have an answer for everything.

You'll be laughing on the other side of your face.

Do you want to see the back of my hand?

I'll give you something to cry for.

You're not too old to go over my knee.

Don't Go Out With Someone You Feel Sorry For
When Di started her periods Muth sat her down and said, 'Don't let anyone put his hands down your knickers. And never go out with anyone you feel sorry for.'

How Do You Do What You Do to Me?
Before Muth had Di and Owen she was Audrey. After leaving school she worked in a greengrocers. She'd wanted to go to secretarial college but her mother said there was no point when she'd only get married and have kids.

Audrey went to Weston-super-Mare for a Bank Holiday weekend with her friend Christine. She took her new one-piece bathing costume bought in the Summer Sales. They met two fellas, Peter and Charlie. Brothers, they said. From Salford they said. Near Manchester. Georgie Best, they said.

Charlie looked a lot like Georgie Best. Peter more like Freddy out of Freddy and the Dreamers. They bought the girls Cinzano and lemonades.

Audrey couldn't stop looking at Charlie. His green eyes, jet-black hair, overlapping front teeth. He made her feel all funny inside and down there. She didn't have the right words for any of this. When his hand brushed her arm, she tingled. Even remembering it years later, she tingled.

Peter and Charlie were in a caravan. Four-berth. We've got ale, they said. They put the radio on. *How do you do what you do to me. I wish I knew.* They danced, staggering and swaying, ricocheting one side of the caravan to the other.

Audrey woke up more or less naked with Charlie. Christine was in the other berth. Peter in a blanket on the floor. After scalding tea and bacon baps, Charlie scribbled a phone number on a bit of card ripped off his fag packet.

Weeks later when Audrey was late she called the number. Peter answered. 'I'm on the next bus down,' he said.

Knickerbocker Glory

For Di's fourteenth birthday Muth took her to a Wimpy bar for a Knickerbocker Glory. Swivelling bar-stools. Glace cherries. Long-stemmed spoons. Ice-cream and peaches bulging her cheeks. On the bar's Formica top, an ashtray. A cigarette butt imprinted with red lip-stick. A chocolate-brown cigar stub. Side by side in a shallow bed of ash. A glimpse of unimaginable glamour.

She Did, She Really Did

Her teachers told Muth Di was bright. Brainy. She could go to Uni, they said. Even Medical school, they said. Muth thought Di's brains must be why she always seemed to have something on her mind. Ever since she was little. Muth could tell. She'd scrunch up her toes so her slippers fell off.

Muth failed the eleven-plus twice. Nerves. She was so shaky she couldn't hold her pen. At the secondary modern, she auditioned for the school musical production: Calamity Jane. She got the main part.

'No,' her mother said. 'You don't want to be prancing about on a stage. Rehearsing all hours.'

But she did, she really did.

You're So Different To Your Sister

At fifteen Owen's hair turned the blondest blonde. His eyes got even bluer. He shot up to nearly six foot. Girls looked at him. An older boy touched his bum. He liked it.

He got a set of hair-clippers. Number two at the sides, number three on top. A load of gel to spike it up. He wanted to go to Art School. Or catering college. Di would probably be a doctor. Or a lawyer.

'You're so different to your sister,' Muth said.

He knew that. One: he knew how to get round Muth. Two: he wasn't a virgin.

Lookout Lookout Lookout Lookout

Muth liked a view, a proper vista. If she ever went on holiday abroad a view would be essential. She'd heard of people getting a room facing a wall. That'd be no good. It'd force her to look in. Into her own mind. And if she did that too long she'd start thinking things. Feeling things.

She'd always pushed feelings down, imagined them as dark shapes with jagged edges. Lurking in the pits of her. Heavy. Hard. If you sliced her in half they'd come banging and clattering to the floor. So she needed to look out.

Lookout Lookout Lookout Lookout.

She was barely eighteen when she had Diana. Owen thirteen months later. She tried her best to look out for them. She knew she didn't always get it right. She knew it was important to try. That was the difference between her and her own mother.

Her brothers didn't speak to her since their mother's funeral. Because of the red shoes.

'Not right,' they said. 'Disrespectful.'

Well they could sod off. They'd never looked out for her.

Common side-effects of Mirtazapine

Drowsiness, dizziness; lethargy; constipation; severe sedation; increased appetite; weight gain; insomnia, fatigue; strange dreams; increased serum cholesterol; vision changes; xerostomia.

'What the hell's xerostomia?' Owen said, looking up from the list of side-effects.

'Dry mouth,' Di said.

'Why the fuck don't they just say that, then?'

I Haven't Been Entirely Straight

Muth said she had to see both of them. She didn't want to discuss it on the phone. Di drove from London and Owen took the train from Brighton.

'Hi darlings.' Muth sat them in the front room. On the coffee table: an opened bottle of Tesco Merlot, three glasses, olives and paper napkins with holly on. Muth was wearing eye-shadow, slightly more on one side. Owen poured the wine.

'Thanks darling,' she said.

Di caught Owen's eye. They both knew all the darlings and the eye-shadow meant Muth was nervous.

'My Will,' she said, 'is straightforward. Sell the house and split the money.'

'Fine,' they said.

'There's something else,' she said. 'Something I, well. I haven't been entirely straight with you about your father.'

Do You Ever Feel Life's Not Worth Living?
Do you ever feel life's not worth living?
Have you ever considered harming yourself?
Have you got as far as making plans?
Have you ever actually tried to harm yourself?

I've thought of it doctor, but I couldn't do that to my kids.
I've thought of it doctor, but I wouldn't have the nerve.
I've thought of it doctor, but I would probably fuck that up as well.

Did He Buy A Single Or A Return?
Di cancelled her clinic, took the tube to Victoria, bought a ticket.

Did he buy a single or a return?

She found an emptyish carriage and slid into a window-seat, sipped her black Americano. So hot it nearly took the roof of her mouth off. She found half a fluffy Kit-Kat in the bowels of her bag.

What did he eat last?

The train slipped across the river, past the butchering of Battersea Power Station, glided above the red-brick red-bus High Streets that slice through South London. Beyond East Croydon, narrow gardens ran down to the track, all patios, plastic furniture, trampolines, and sheds erected at weekends from flat-packs.

They sped up as suburbs thinned and green began beneath a broadening sky. A man in waders stood with a rod in a pond. An England flag the size of a house flapped on a village green. Kids on bikes, dogs, and a woman with a shopping trolley waited at a level crossing. The sweep of the south Downs, then, Sainsbury's, Currys, PC World: the outskirts of it-could-be–anywhere:

'*This is Eastbourne, your final station stop. Southern Trains apologises for the delay to your service today. This is due to ongoing train crew issues.*'

She walked from the station, blinking in the sun. People wore stripy t-shirts, carried stripy towels in stripy bags on their shoulders. She'd forgotten how the seaside brought people out in stripes. She crossed to the beach. *Did he do the same, or go straight up?* The Pier lunged out on black laddered legs, its shimmering white pavilion topped with domes of gold and silver. All around the whoosh of the tide, the piercing whine of gulls. *Did he hear any of this?*

She followed the rust-coloured path westward past a Bowling Club, a private school, and a café at the bottom of the cliff, where she steeled herself, and leaned into the slope, a warm breeze on her face. Where the path widened and the incline softened she looked back. Her gut lurched. She was giddily high already. The wind was keener, cooler, the drone of traffic dimmer but for the odd revving of motorbikes. At a fork she went right. *Which did he take?*

A sign warned, '*Watch Out Walkers*' in a meadow full of buttercups and tiny blue flowers she couldn't remember the name of but thought might be forget-me-nots. The sea appeared ahead, baby-boy blue beyond the cliff edge. Signs on battered planks nailed to posts just the right height to trip people up said: *CLIFF EDGE,* and *DANGER: CLIFF EROSION.*

She craned to glimpse the chalky white crumble of the cliff face. It sloped away so she couldn't see the beach below. If she leaned far enough to see that she'd be over. If you could look, you could leap. Five hundred and thirty-one feet of cliff, cliff ready to batter flesh, smash bones, bounce and toss a body. She imagined pulverised organs, shit and entrails splattered everywhere. She'd read in the paper a dog chasing a seagull went over. It was running so fast it overshot the cliff, hit the sea at high tide, and survived.

Did he take a run?

Engraved on a stone several feet from the edge:

Psalm 93, verse 4

Mightier than the thunders of many waters,

Mightier than the waves of the sea,

The Lord on high is mighty

He had no time for God.

She took in the soaring sky, the vistas oozing metaphor. Opportunity. Reinvention. New horizons.

Had none of it spoken to him?

Beachy Head: from the French, *beau chef*, meaning beautiful headland. She'd looked it up. It was nothing to do with beach. To her east, the sulphurous haze *of* Hastings. To the west, The Seven Sisters. And he'd had just one.

When he hadn't returned her texts, emails or calls she'd phoned his office. They hadn't seen him in three weeks, they said. That wasn't unusual, they said. It was news to her. So was the drink-driving charge. And that his boyfriend had left him to go back to an ex-lover in Brazil.

Pinned to the stop as she waited for the bus back to Eastbourne, a notice: *The Samaritans, Always There Day and Night, Call 116123 (free).*

His body has not been found.

James Kennedy

James Kennedy was born and raised in London and read PPE at Oxford. A 'portfolio' career has taken him through stints in banking, consultancy and market research. He came to writing relatively late and is currently completing an MA in Creative Writing at Birkbeck, University of London. James's writing is inspired by coastal Suffolk which has been his home for the last four years.

Autumn Colours

You'd have loved the autumn colours. The leaves on the Spanish chestnuts have just begun to turn. You'd have had a name for that particular shade of yellow – somewhere between lemon and gold – but I'm afraid I don't. It's been warm and dry and there's a sweetness in the air I've not noticed before at this time of year. So different from last October when we had all of that rain.

I've spent the day clearing out your studio. A year on and it's the first time I've been in there. I can't believe how much you kept: every doodle and daub from the Slade and before. Did you really imagine people would be interested? It's been hard work sorting through it, but I'm getting there. Danny's here and he's been looking through some of the portfolios. I know you wouldn't approve, but he has a far better eye than you gave him credit for.

There's a vigour in some of your early oils and I love your use of red. I think you'd almost stopped using it by the time we met and your canvasses had started to shrink. I wasn't aware of it then, but you were already past your peak. It's a shame: the arrogance of your early work is compelling.

Watercolour never really was your medium. Yes, I know people liked them, and they're easy to live with, but would you really want your work thought decorative? They're too polite, and not at all like the real you.

Better to focus on the oils and the charcoals. You know, you really could draw. I'd forgotten. There's a series of nudes I'm particularly taken with. The model's a touch Neanderthal, but there's an undeniable masculinity that gives the studies a tension often missing from your work. Danny asked if the model had been your lover. I can hear you laugh, but it gave me an idea; you know how people like a story. I got a bit carried away and ended up telling him all about your love life, except it wasn't yours at all. Still, my version's a lot more colourful; I think you'd have been amused.

Danny wondered why there was nothing of me, not even a sketch. I'd never really thought about it and didn't know what to say. 'You have an interesting profile' – wasn't that the first thing you ever said to me? I think that might be the closest you ever came to paying me a compliment.

The artist beginning to emerge from our efforts is impressive; we're already talking about a show. Somewhere in Dalston with brushed concrete floors and industrial lighting; very different from that place on the Fulham Road where you had your last one. Danny says we'll be saving you from obscurity and that you'd thank us.

Yesterday afternoon we drove out to Rendelsham Forest. We parked in that little lay-by and wandered through the birches. I was warm enough in the dappled shade in just a t-shirt and shorts. It's funny, but it wasn't until we reached the little clearing where you and I saw the white thirteen-pointer that I realised that was where it had happened. It's been so dry that the fragile filigree of the bracken remains uncrushed and lurking beneath there's a prodigious crop of fungi. Danny said what a great place it would be to forage and then looked over at me as he remembered. I did my best to look sad and we walked on, his arm around my shoulder. Having him here has been such a comfort.

I'd warned you before about picking mushrooms but you'd brushed aside my townie concerns. Even if I'd said something then, would you have listened? Not listening was quite a thing of yours. 'One-way traffic', Celia said about your tendency to monopolise the conversation. Oh yes, I've become quite a regular up at the big house and they've taken quite a shine to Danny; the other day, Richard even referred to him as my partner. I know we're invited over there to add colour and to amuse the Aldeburgh crowd, but old Dicky's not quite the reactionary you had pegged him for. They must have seen through the whole 'studio assistant' routine years ago; why did you insist on keeping up the pretence? They seemed amazed that you and I were together for seventeen years; amazed, I think, that anyone could have put up with you for that long.

I watched you pick each mushroom, wipe it clean of dirt and place it carefully in that ridiculous little basket you bought at the flower show after you'd claimed the prize for my roses. At one with nature, or so you must have thought; a personal communion borne of breeding and your own artistic sensibility. But I gleaned more from the *Spotter's Guide to Mushrooms and Toadstools* than you ever managed from umpteen generations of country gentlefolk; I knew a death cap when I saw one. To be fair, they do look rather innocuous and I find something to admire in their understatement. The gills are pure white and appetizing but if you look closely you'll see that the caps themselves have a greenish hue. So often the colour of harmony, green here warns of amatoxins, poisonous in even the smallest quantities and thermostable, so their toxic effects aren't reduced when you cook them. Greed must have got the better of your sharp eye that day and you carried on picking.

I could have said something when we got home. Maybe printed something off the Internet; but even then would you have believed me? You'd have accused me of making a fuss, and that was always your prerogative, especially after you'd had a glass or six. Heaven forfend that I should put a foot wrong, mispronounce a word, say the wrong thing; thirteen years since I'd asked Lizzy Graham-Watson for a 'serviette' and still you couldn't let it drop. It was late, too late for tea. What was that you used to say about tea-making being vulgar except between four and six? And I had choir to go to.

I looked on as you heated the smallest copper skillet, melted rather too much butter and added the mushrooms. You crushed and added two cloves of garlic and maybe even a third; you always used a lot and it would have overwhelmed the flavour of the fungi. You chopped a handful of flat-leaf parsley in that chef-y way you'd seen on TV and sprinkled it over the plated mushrooms. I can't remember you even offering me a taste, but if you had, the sheer quantity of garlic was all the excuse I'd have needed. I remember the church bell chiming the half hour as I left; I was late for practise and Godfrey was cross, but I needed to see that first forkful pass your lips. We rehearsed the *Ave Verum* and I was complimented on my singing. I never did understand how you could not like Mozart.

I remember opening the front door and wondering what I would find. The sight of you slumped in the drawing room brought a momentary frisson but then you stirred, asked what was for supper and had the gall to complain that my pea and ham risotto wouldn't be a match for the amarone you'd opened. You must have attributed the stomach ache you were complaining of to hunger because you ate with abandon, in spite of the too wet rice and inferior parmesan. What got me through the meal was knowing that it was quite possibly your last. You polished off the wine and fell asleep on the sofa as I cleared up; each of your snores telling me I'd done the right thing. I slept in the little bedroom – that was how it had been for some time – and when I left the next morning a bestial cacophony was still reverberating through the house; all the effort we put into curing your sleep apnoea had been a complete waste.

I was meeting a new client on the other side of Woodbridge; weekenders from London busily removing any trace of rural charm from their Victorian rectory. They'd engaged me to design a new garden; all box hedges, pleached beeches and raked gravel. You despised my 'trade', but I'm a working breed and it gave me time out of the house. Besides, we needed the money; heirlooms don't pay bills. Danny, by the way, is full of admiration for my ability to transform a space and I've got some exciting plans for the garden, after we've converted your studio into a new guest suite. I'd put my phone on silent and the meeting went on longer than expected – you know how demanding Islingtonians can be – so it must have been half eleven by the time I checked and saw the voicemails you'd left. Your voice echoing around the bathroom accompanied by unfortunate sound effects; you must have been in some distress.

I stopped off in Wooders to pick up a few things and arrived home to find that nice young doctor from the Peninsular practice in attendance. Given the state you'd left the bathroom in, his diagnosis of a norovirus seemed eminently plausible, as was his desire not to have you admitted to hospital where you might have infected other patients and undermined an already over-stretched NHS. The pills he gave you calmed things down and you fell into a deep sleep. I'd hoped that might have been the end of it; things having already taken rather longer than anticipated. The thought of Googling crossed my mind, but online searches can be so incriminating. The only thing was to wait it out, so I busied myself around the house before sitting down with the latest Patrick Gale; it's a shame you never got around to reading it, it's very much your kind of thing. I checked in on you around seven and you were still asleep; silent, which was a little eerie, but definitely not dead. I made myself supper and sat down to watch something dreadful on TV. I know you disapprove of meals on knees but it had been a long day and I was tired.

I was awoken by the awful wailing coming from upstairs. You weren't making any sense and the only thing for it was to dial 999. The ambulance got here in under half an hour; all the way from Ipswich, which is pretty impressive. I don't get why people are always complaining about the decline in rural services. There was a look in your eyes as they loaded you into the ambulance; I don't think I'll ever be able to forget it.

I followed on behind as they took you to the hospital. It's not where you'd have imagined spending your final hours, but the nurses were friendly and they found you your own room; being on a large ward really would have been too awful. It was a while before they let me see you. The rather good-looking Italian doctor told me that you were suffering multiple organ failure – heart, liver, kidneys – and warned me to expect the worst. Nothing, however, could have prepared me for the sight greeting me as I entered your room. Between your being loaded into the ambulance and my seeing you in the hospital, your body had become entirely jaundiced; the colour of your flesh a match for the fading red of your hair. You looked like a corpulent version of Ginger in the British Museum. My distress at seeing you was very real and I'm thankful you never had to look at yourself in that state. Tubes emerged from every orifice, though why, I'm not too sure, as the staff were at great pains to impress on me the impossibility of recovery. In the event, you managed to linger on until a quarter to five, and I found myself driving home along a deserted A12 early on a wet Wednesday morning in October.

I've always loved the point where you turn off the Bromeswell Roundabout and you really know you're on the road home but that morning I had no sense of homecoming. There was a low mist over the B1083 that didn't lift until Chillesford and that was when it hit me: the enormity of what had happened. Up until that point it had felt like a game

– one I'd actually succeeded in winning.

Danny, ever the dutiful godson, came up from London as soon as he heard. He stayed on to help with the arrangements and never really went back. I know what you're thinking, but there'd been nothing going on between us. There was a moment that time in Ravello, but I never pursued it. Your leaving him the house came as a great surprise, to both of us. Would I have done what I did if I'd known? I'm not sure it would have made a difference; I wasn't calculated about what happened, not in that way. I just needed it all to end.

Your not leaving me anything was actually a blessing. On the road from Chillesford it suddenly hit me how much I owed you; I do believe my life with you was better than the one I'd have had if we'd never met. But the knowledge that you'd have allowed everything to be taken away from me wiped away all feelings of gratitude.

Danny told me how awkward it made him feel – his owning my home of so many years – and insisted on placing it in both our names. He really is a sweet boy and you were right about his lack of guile; he wouldn't have lasted five minutes growing up on the streets of Lewisham. I can hear you muttering about the age difference but it's the same as the gap between you and me. I do miss the challenge – you always were that – but he's great company and the house fills with voices and laughter.

Your funeral was well-attended. Mostly locals, but some of the old London gang were there. I called Molly but she was still angry and none of the other cousins were keen; I suppose it was asking quite a lot after what happened in Italy. You know how the vicar loves his bells and smells; I think some of the congregation may have mistaken you for a late-in-life left-footer. I went with the Missa Brevis; we'd been rehearsing it for Snape and it seemed a shame not to try it out. The sound was lovely and quite brought a tear to the eye. I've always found that church a little stark but Jeanette and the other ladies covered it in dahlias and chrysanths in an explosion of seasonal vulgarity which you'd have loathed. I couldn't face having people back to the house, not with the upstairs loo still out of action, so we had the wake in the village hall, and Joan from The Crown provided finger food. She did the whole thing gratis; claimed she'd always known you'd had a heart of gold. She obviously never heard what you'd said about her fish pie.

I found myself talking to Rob Benarcek. I'd forgotten you'd been at art school together. He said you were quite the tyro, of whom great things were expected, leaving chaos in your wake. You never spoke about the sixties, or the seventies for that matter. I sensed your discomfort and didn't probe. Rob told me about California; I knew you'd been, but had no idea you'd lived there three years. Late seventies San Francisco – that's a part of you I'd like to have known better. I always thought you hated dancing. He's sold the agency but still leads a very active life; did you know he was on the board of the Whitechapel? You don't have to be old at sixty-six.

I had you cremated, by the way. I got a quote for lifting the lid off the vault and the cost really was prohibitive. Besides, I can't imagine you'd really be happy in there lying next to your father and your poor mother. Your ashes are still sitting in an urn in the shed while I make up my mind what to do with them. Danny suggested Dunwich and I'm coming around to the idea; you liked it there and there's something oddly appropriate about your final resting place being a town that was lost beneath the waves. We'll need to pick a day with a strong westerly.

Amanda O'Callaghan

Amanda O'Callaghan's short stories and flash fiction have been published and won awards in Australia, UK, and Ireland. A former advertising executive, she has a BA and MA in English from King's College, London. She holds a PhD in English from the University of Queensland. Amanda recently won the Bath Flash Fiction Award. She lives in Brisbane, Australia, where she is completing her first collection of stories. More details about her work can be found at www.amandaocallaghan.com

Things

There are no neighbours. That's important. Old Mr Novak, who lived for decades on the other side of our walls, is long gone. I still miss hearing snatches of his beautiful baritone, and, just once, late at night, a heartbreaking violin, never repeated. When I mentioned this he shook his head and said, "No, no, my dear, there was no violin. It must have been the radio," and asked about my sister. I told him Lottie was fine, and changed the subject. But after all the years separated by a narrow seam of brick and ageing plaster, I knew his bedroom was the mirror image of my own. The sound of the violin was unmistakeable. No matter. We all have our secrets.

I have only three houses to consider. Our house, which is the end one, once belonged to a typically English terrace of red-brick homes, all curving slightly to the left like a wheeling regiment of soldiers. Our parents had just moved in when German bombers reduced two of the houses and their occupants to orange rubble. The gap remains, filled by a half-hearted children's play area. Mr Novak's place is still empty. While his nephews wrangle over their inheritance, the house waits quietly, unperturbed, its window blinds firmly down.

The third house in our truncated row is also empty, but not for long. It's just been sold. There's an article in the local newspaper, here in front of me. A neat young man in a buttoned-up shirt, smiling into the camera.

Chess prodigy makes a move on renovation. There's new blood coming into the neighbourhood, a sense of all that is old and dull being swept away. Cleansed. This is entirely right.

Our house was big, once. Especially the front room, with its bay window and a great square rug, wide enough to lie across. One year, when Lottie and I were small, we had a Christmas tree in the far corner. The last of its trunk is in the back garden somewhere.

By the time Lottie was seventeen, there was still a little bit of space left in the front room. I remember her sitting in there, in the window, perched on the arm-rest of the old navy sofa. That year, the local school band was playing across the street, collecting money in a woven basket. A sign on the grass verge explained that they were saving for a coach trip to London. Carols. It didn't feel cold enough for Christmas carols. The snow came much later that winter. The snow that changed everything.

I can still picture Lottie watching passers-by gravitate towards the band. "They're putting money in the basket, Jenny," she told me. She was pleased, but she was getting over-excited. She said she could see the mean woman. That was the old hag from the sweet shop. Lottie had gone in there once, but she got her words into a muddle and the woman wouldn't serve her. "I can't make out what you're saying," she said to her. She told her to come back with a responsible adult.

"Look, Jenny, look!" Lottie called out, that day. When I went to the window, I could see the sweet shop woman hanging back, one misshapen arm holding onto a wrought-iron fence. She kept so many tissues balled in her cardigan sleeves that they looked like tumours under the wool.

"She's getting music for free!" Lottie was shouting and pointing. "She's stealing it!"

I told Lottie there was no rule about having to give money, that it was voluntary, but she started jumping on the sofa, yelling "Stealing,

stealing" until I came and calmed her. I remember she was wearing our grandmother's necklace. A heavy gold chain with a crescent moon pendant, its inner curve edged with tiny red stones. As Lottie jumped and shouted, the chain flew up, its bright paring of moon suspended, for a moment, before she fell to earth again.

"Indian rubies," our grandmother had told us in a whispery voice, when we'd first seen that necklace. "My wedding present from your dear grandfather."

Lottie and I had watched, transfixed, as the gaudy moon bobbed under her fingers. After Grandma died, our mother said, "Garnets, if they're real stones at all" and dropped the necklace into a box of old, broken toys on the hall table. She had a way of pulling the air out of a room, of filling it to the brim with negative things.

After the band played on the corner, Lottie never went into the front room again. A young couple with heavy shopping bags had stopped at the gate to rearrange their parcels. They noticed Lottie waving and calling out. But the couple seemed to sense something wasn't right and the man put his arm around the woman and turned her away. Poor Charlotte got very upset then. It was too much for her. I made her stay in the back kitchen after that. She could be peaceful there.

The old sofa is still in the front room, though I haven't seen it for years. There's no view from the window anymore. Not long ago I squeezed in there, and I could hear children outside, bouncing a ball. There was something about those sounds: the slap, slap of the rubber on the pavement, a screechy girl, the way another one laughed – a big, throaty laugh – that reminded me of Lottie. I felt too sad to be standing there, so I worked my way back to the hall, pulling the door behind me as much as I could. I won't go in there again. It will be like Mr Novak's house, like our parents' room, like Lottie's room: places that have closed their eyes forever.

Lottie is dead. She was always so vibrant and dramatic that it's hard, even now, to accept how plain her death was. There was no rare and terrible disease, no violence, no deadly sting from a creature that had sailed halfway around the world in the nib of a banana. If I had known how awful a plain death could be, I would have wished for some glossy black spider to find its poisonous way in here. Make it quick.

When the snow finally came that year, it filled the back garden, softening the boxy edges of things into something less jagged and imposing. It piled up on the front path, clouded the windows, muffled the grind of the town. We were cocooned here, and quite calm. There was always food. The pipes froze, but we had boxes of bottled water that had been stacked in the pantry when our parents were alive. Towards the end of that week, someone made their way to our front door and knocked for a long time. I think they may have pushed something through the letterbox. Later, from the corner of an upstairs window, we could see the way the snow on the front path had been trampled and pushed aside. We both stared when we saw the old wooden gate left open to the street.

Lottie loved winter. Even when she was a small child she never seemed to feel the cold. I can barely recall her wearing a coat, or gloves. She hated the heat. When she was about eleven, there was a very hot summer. One long, stifling night she called out repeatedly from her bed, "Too hot. No air," and banged on the wall with the flat of her hand.

She was so happy when the big snow came. Gusts of wind drove it onto the windows, where it splattered against the glass like the limbs of some flying insect. Sometimes it fell straight down, silent and endless. Lottie was mesmerised. There was a high, narrow window in the back kitchen with one of the big dining room chairs underneath it. Lottie would teeter on the pile of newspapers stacked there, watching the snow fall in the back garden.

"Charlotte, get down and pull that window closed," I'd tell her. "There's a terrible draught."

But Lottie would push her face through the small opening and gulp in the freezing air, trying to catch flakes of snow on her tongue. She'd stand on that chair for hours at a time. It was becoming harder to keep her calm. It sometimes suited me to leave her there, her face glowing and ruddy with cold.

It began with the heating oil men. Two of them: one not much older than Lottie, the other middle-aged. "Did you see the state of the place?" I heard the young one say. "Christ, how does anyone live like that?"

The older man was pulling the oil hose back towards the truck. "Nutters," he said. "And my old girl thinks I'm bad. Can't wait to tell her about this lot."

I was standing at the dining room window, listening to every word they said. They couldn't see me with all the boxes stacked against the glass. The boxes were empty; I'd been keeping them for the local kindergarten. I could hear the men outside, breathing in the cold air, the hose dragging on the ground.

"You'll need to get a signature," I heard the older man say. "Go to the back door," he said. "The older one is half normal. Here, take my pen. You'll be drawing the pension before they can find one in that mess."

The younger man, whose top teeth were bucked, was still chuckling when he appeared at the door. I signed without saying a word. Lottie was calling out, "Thank you, thank you, oil man," from the hallway.

"You'll be nice and snug now," he said to me, kindly enough, before closing the folder. But I heard them laughing as they went back down the path. The sound of the truck roaring away left a mark on my heart.

The buck-toothed boy was right: we were nice and snug that winter. Just me and Lottie, curled like hedgehogs in our chairs. We had everything we needed in that back kitchen. We boiled the eggs that Mr Novak left for us in a padded bag by the side gate. We had our beans, and I found some lime cordial that Lottie would have drunk neat if I hadn't stopped her. I'd given up buying the newspaper by then, but I had a tiny radio that I listened to when the gales were blowing. *Rockall, Hebrides. Becoming cyclonic. Bailey. Fair Isle. Cyclonic at times.* The thought of those turbulent places, the unstoppable, chaotic forces sweeping across them, was oddly soothing. It was the hardest winter for seventy years the radio told me: motorways were closed, there were pile-ups, people stranded in freezing cars. Watching Lottie beside me, sleeping peacefully in her chair, made me feel lucky, for a while.

Sometimes terrible mistakes only become clear later, when everything is lost. This old house has two floors, three if you count the attic, although I haven't been able to get up there for years. When it got so cold that even Lottie was starting to feel the chill, I turned the heating up to maximum without a thought. Much later, I realised every radiator in the house was going at full tilt, warming rooms we'd not been in for years. Even the attic must have had some sort of heating because I've never seen so many birds in our back garden, swooping down onto the icy branches of trees, then back up to the warm slate of our roof. Dozens of them. Hundreds.

It's surprising how quickly a house goes cold. And the quiet that comes when the dull throb of the machinery ceases. The birds left first. A large flock curved above Mr Novak's house, then disappeared. Lottie didn't complain, even though she pulled out an old school cardigan of mine and wrapped it around her neck like a scarf. I told her there was no oil left. "Get the man," she said. The young fellow had grinned at her with his huge teeth and she had not forgotten. But I kept hearing their laughter on the side path, kept seeing their faces at the back door. How their eyes had widened in surprise, the shocked glance the two exchanged before turning to their work.

The empty house beside Mr Novak's old place was once a teacher's house. He was no relation to us although we shared the same family name. "Looks like this is going to be the Greene end of the Terrace," the postman, who was universally known as Call-me-Johnny, sang out as I passed one day. He'd been ringing the front doorbell but getting no answer. "Another Greene just moved in here, by the looks of it," he said to me. "Unless of course you've got a..." – he read the label – "...Simon Greene tucked up in your place, Jennifer?"

"I'm afraid that's me." A middle-aged man in a pale blue shirt appeared at the door, looking slightly flustered. "Sorry, I was in the back garden," he said.

"There's Greene everywhere!" Call-me-Johnny said, quite delighted with his silly quips. He pointed to me. "This lady's Greene, too; lives two doors up."

I was eager to get away but the man took the parcel and stepped down to the front gate to introduce himself.

"Delighted to meet you," he said, as we exchanged names and shook hands. He had a pair of reading glasses tucked into his shirt pocket. He nodded at the parcel he'd pinned under one arm. "Another book," he said, ruefully. "Don't seem to be able to resist." He had dark brown hair, cut quite short, except for a long sweep of fringe with a couple of strands of silvery grey. "I'll have to cut back on my addiction now that I've bought this place." He had a nice voice.

"Oh blimey, not another book lover!" The postman was still standing beside us. "You'll be the death of me, you lot," he said, staggering on the footpath in mock horror, before chuckling to himself and walking away, patting his heavy satchel like the head of a large dog.

We laughed then, the two of us, new neighbours and soon to be friends. Just a few years after that, books would be ordered online and exhausted couriers in lurid trucks would ply this road. Call-Me-Johnny, finding nothing funny in his new work contract, would take voluntary redundancy and retire to Blackpool. But the first time I met Simon is set fast in my mind. The two of us smiling, watching the postman make his way down the terrace, Simon's hand on the gatepost, the wrapped book under his arm. And the way we said, "Yes, an amazing coincidence... common enough name, for sure, but still." And how we talked about books, then, free-falling into that vast canopy of stories. "Oh yes, I've read it," and, "I was a little disappointed with her last novel but I just couldn't put her new one down," and, "Absolutely, an incredible story; I was crying by the end of it. It was brilliant. Just brilliant."

If I could choose my final thought on this earth, it would be that scene, for the innocent happiness it brought me. The two of us, together, smiling. When I think of it, I am a shining, iridescent creature, caught with him forever in smooth amber. Extinguished, yet perfect.

Someone was at the front door, knocking. I wasn't afraid. It was not unusual for charity collectors or other strangers to let themselves into the front garden. I ignored it, as I always do. That door hasn't been opened for years.

Strange how people who want something always knock the same way: three assertive knocks, silence, two more knocks, silence. After a long pause, I'd hear the gate creak, then nothing. When I think back on it, the knocks I heard that day were different: more tentative, uncertain. But then the silence came, and I relaxed again.

A few minutes later, I heard footsteps. Someone was walking down the path at the side of the house. Even then, I was unconcerned. I was in my chair in the back kitchen. I won't make a sound, I thought. No one can see me from here.

But then I remembered the robin. It was an unusually warm day. Early autumn. A robin had perched on the old washing machine outside. I had watched it for a long time. It didn't move, just tilted its plain head to and fro, its red chest flaring in the light.

I had left the back door open. The footsteps rounded the corner of the house.

"Jennifer? Hello. Jennifer? Are you there?"

The voice was unmistakable. It was Simon. I felt a cymbal crash of panic shoot through my body. If he moved any closer to the door, he would see me.

He was wearing the same blue shirt he'd had on when we first met. He smiled when he spotted me. I treasure that. He had a parcel in his hand, clearly a book.

"Jennifer!" he said in a pleased, slightly relieved voice. And then he said, "Oh!" loud and fast, stepping back from the doorway as if the threshold were an unexpected cliff. His free hand slapped against his throat but it was too late to trap the sound of his shock.

For one precious moment, he had seen only me. Then he saw everything else. And it was just like the oil men, the way his eyes took in all the things. Without moving, without so much as turning my head, I saw what he saw. He was breathing like a man who had run a long way.

"I'm so sorry," he said, quietly. He held up the parcel. "The postman. Got it wrong. Wrong Greene, I mean." He took another small step backwards. "It's a book. I... I didn't mean to intrude."

I stood up. We faced each other on either side of the doorway. Simon was forcing his gaze away from the room and back to my face.

"I thought I'd leave this by the back door but then... I saw... it was open," he said, his face blazing.

I felt a surge of absolute fury. I wanted to step across that threshold and pummel him, rip that book apart and grind it under my shoe. He had wrecked everything by coming here. I'd played a careful game. Small deceptions that meant we met in the street, or in a cafe, or at the library. I'd had coffee in his house. I told him an ancient aunt of mine lived here, that visitors disturbed her. And it had been wonderful. All those stories, those books. We'd built great walls of book talk around us. There was no romance. I wondered a few times whether he might be gay. I didn't care. I was glad to have a friend.

I heard myself say, "I don't think you should come here again, Simon."

He pressed his lips together. "No," he said. He cast about briefly for some flat surface to put down the book. There was none. Seeing that, he held it out to me. I took the terrible weight of it in my hand. "I'm so very sorry," he said, before walking away.

I was still standing in the doorway when he reappeared. He stopped a few steps from the back door. I could see the robin on a pile of wood near him. It seemed as if years had passed.

"Jennifer," he said. "I could help you."

It was then I felt it. The terror. I felt those walls of rubbish behind me, above me. All at once they seemed to move, flex, like powerful muscles. Like a house come to life with things. In the maze of boxes, it knew where I was, squeezed into this small corner of kitchen, the door in front of me my last escape. All I had to do was step forward, reach out, cross that threshold. Simon would take my hand. He was a good man. He would help me. But the house, this house I reshaped into something terrible, was contracting against me. Even the floor seemed to wrap around my feet like a sinuous vine.

Simon took a step closer. "I'm worried about you," he said. "Being here. And your aunt. It's not safe."

Despite his best efforts, I saw his eyes flit around the room.

"Jennifer, how would you both get out," he said. "What if something happened? If there was... a fire?"

A fire. And I felt my pulse race, even then. A beautiful, cleansing fire to vanquish this monstrous place.

"There is no aunt," I said. I was amazed to hear my own robot voice.

Simon stared, took a deep breath. "I see," he whispered.

"I don't need any help, thank you, Simon," I told him. I felt a throb of life in the floor beneath me.

He was going to say more, I could see that, but after a moment he lowered his gaze. "Very well," he said. "Jennifer, I'm so sorry I came here. I meant no harm."

It was a strange, courtly end. I would not have been surprised if he'd bowed.

There is no going back. No returning to the Christmas tree, or the navy sofa on the big square rug. No Lottie spinning and jumping, catching snow on her tongue. "So hot," she'd said to me, in those last hours we spent together, the fever boiling within her. I didn't realise how sick she was until I heard the high, thin wheeze of her chest, filled to the brim.

When the ambulance men came, they noticed only Lottie. They did not care about things. They did not look at me. Together, we stared at Lottie, lying limp in her chair. They lifted her up and carried her to the gurney at the door. Pneumonia, they said. Only Lottie looked back, her eyes half closed, willing me to make it better. So hot. No air. The wail of the siren in the street. And then she was gone.

There is no going back. I have built a new house here, with seams of paper and cloth, with walls as thick and heavy as a citadel. There've been times when these narrow corridors, these rooms of things, gave me a kind of comfort, like the books around my bed when I was young.

"You'll disappear under those books, my girl," my mother once said as I lay on the bed, reading.

"She's lost in all those silly stories," I heard her tell my father.

After Lottie died, I became afraid of everything. The books could no longer console me. They loomed at me with their closed mouths, their pressed lips. I put boxes around them, covered them with newspapers. I did not think of Simon. In the local paper, there was a small photo of his house. For sale. A beautifully-kept garden, it said. Tranquil. I thought about that word for a long time. I curled beside the boxes, the tins and jars, the magazines, our old schoolwork, Lottie's clothes tucked in beside me, each garment scented with a ghostly trace of her.

It's astonishing how many boxes of matches are here in this house. Enough to burn the street, the town, the whole world. I light things as I walk. The house feels glad again, released. It hums with the joy of things ending. The hallway opens for me. I take the stairs, climb towards the attic.

Poppy O'Neill

Poppy O'Neill lives in Chichester and runs the Writers' HQ retreat in Portsmouth. Her stories have been published in *Oh Comely*, *Pithead Chapel*, *The Ham* and *The Forgotten and the Fantastical 3* anthology from Mother's Milk Books. She's currently working on her first novel and studying for an MA in Creative Writing at the University of Chichester. Her first book of children's non-fiction will be published by Summersdale in spring 2018.

Skyward!

We are leaving the party: it's grown boring. The slow dances have begun. On the way out you swipe and yank a climbing rose from the veranda, as it unwinds from the pillars it is stripped of its leaves and petals, leaving a barbed vine trailing 15 feet in our wake.

We're running, and laughing, showing our white teeth and fat red tonsils. Hilarious tears run black rivers of mascara down our cheeks.

Thieves! shouts our host from the front door. He has heard the clank of silver in the sack slung over my shoulder.

We scramble into our balloon's basket and you pull the burner valve. The flame roars and singes your horsehair wig. The smell makes me gag and I bring up a tinkly champagne burp.

The balloon inflates, its trompe l'oeil patterns lit from within, and we begin to rise, blowing kisses to the host – red faced and just a moment too late to catch us. You throw him the roses with their long bald stem and thank him for his hospitality by baring your buttocks over the lip of the basket.

We lurch to the height of the rooftop and the wind carries us west. The stars wink and flirt. I loll and flutter back at them from behind an ostrich-feather fan, before flinging it boomerang-style into the night.

"Don't you know," you say, laughing already at your own joke, "ostriches can't fly?" This is the sort of weak witticism we'd boo and armpit-fart at had it come from one of the insufferable fops at the party; but in this dizziest, most drunken night, it brings the house down.

I wiggle a bottle of champagne from the ice trough and squeeze the cork out in your direction, spraying you with bubbles. You cackle, scooping them up and throwing them back at me. After licking your lips and your arms clean, you peer over the edge of the basket and declare us too close to the ground. There's a pine forest swaying in the distance, threatening to tip us out with its witchy black turrets.

"Fire in the hole!" you bellow and crank the flame to its maximum capacity. Still we bob level with the occasional passing farmhouse chimney.

I swig from the bottle and pass it to you, "We'll have to lose something."

Our sandbags are empty, thanks to your seaside-themed New Year's Eve party six months previous. You drain the bottle and toss it overboard, and I follow suit with the rest of the empties, but keep the corkscrew.

"Wigs?" I suggest, worming my finger in to scratch my scalp. We remove them like five-tiered wedding cakes, revealing our gleaming, porkish baldness. They drop to the ground with twin thuds.

Turkish delight, German sausage and unopened bills litter the countryside as we shed weight gram by gram. The ice trough lands with a rattle of cubes.

Soon we are down to our chemises and bloomers, our dresses floating like ghosts pursued by peep-toed missiles. Our corsets flap their whale-bone wings, making their way back east. The pines loom ahead. The fire sputters and dies.

I hadn't noticed what a racket the burners had been making. Now we are bathed in eery quiet. The wind and God's good graces keep us afloat. You pull the sack of silver from under me. Cold air snakes and tickles through the gaps in the wicker. I shake my head: the silver is ours.

You hold me in a steady stare. I lunge for the sack but you're quicker than me. You haul it over the edge and jerk its dull contents free. Knives and forks and candlesticks pierce the soft earth like misfired arrows.

I can smell the forest now, and we are not going to make it. You say nothing. We kiss thirstily, saying goodbye to those parts of our bodies we'll miss most. We hold hands, our cocktail rings knock together, our teeth chatter. We leap from the edge.

The basket tips and gasps as it hits the trees. The silk balloon swoons gracefully over the dense greenness.

We die noisily in some damp-fallowed field at the edge of the forest. You and I, and the mechanical whir of geese passing overhead. I glimpse the stars – stitched with such care across the wide clear sky. They were never winking at us; it was only their light stumbling on its way to earth. I wonder why we left the party in the first place, when there are so many worse things in this life than a slow dance.

Joanna Quinn

Joanna Quinn is a fiction writer with a background in journalism. Her stories have been published by *The White Review*, *New Welsh Review* and The Bridport Prize. She was chosen as an emerging writer as part of the Arvon/Jerwood Mentoring Scheme and shortlisted for the national Arts Foundation Fellowship for Short Stories. Her most recent publications include a story shortlisted for The White Review Short Story Prize 2015 and a commissioned story for art project Flood House. She has also written about Greenham Common for Comma Press. She lives in Dorset and is working towards a PhD in Creative Writing at Goldsmiths.

The Lost Kings of Somerset

The children summoned me, banging at my front door loud enough to raise the dead.

"Mum's at a silent retreat in Yeovil but she got her dates wrong and won't be back til tomorrow," announced Willow, the eldest, in the heraldic manner of a child entrusted with an important message.

"How has she conveyed this information?" I asked. "Mime?"

"Text," said Bear the middle child, without looking up from the gaming console he was attacking with alternate thumbs.

"We've got a babysitter til five but mum wants you to stay overnight on the sofa bed, Uncle Claude. She says soz for late notice," said Willow, still loudly in charge. "We haven't had any tea."

"Goodness. If she says 'soz', how can I refuse? I'll bring you an Indian feast of my own creation."

The children exchanged pleased glances, Bear momentarily letting go of his bleeping device to perform a brief fist-pump.

"Naan or rice?" I asked.

"Naan," they replied in unison.

"Keema or Peshwari? Why do I even ask the question? Always Peshwari. And chicken korma for the young King Arthur."

Valentine, the youngest, pulled his thumb from his mouth with a wet pop. "Chicken for Arfur," he echoed happily.

The children and I have a conceit, you see. I do not refer to them by their ludicrous given names. Last year, when they and their mother and their cat moved next door and I was first co-opted into looking after them, they badgered me to tell them stories. I recited tales from my own area of interest – King Arthur and the Knights of the Round Table – rather than slog through some nonsense about anthropomorphic trains. To their surprise, they rather enjoyed this, and now have their own Arthurian nicknames. Willow is Guinevere. Bear is Merlin. Young Valentine, Arthur himself.

They suit their names. Nine-year-old Guinevere has a rather patrician self-importance, while seven-year-old Merlin is studiously intense. And chubby Arthur, just three years old – well, it has often struck me there is something kingly about toddlers: their autocratic fury and then their sudden tender concern – small boneless hands patting your knees kindly. Pat pat pat. Something felt as a great gift. The king's favour.

So later that day, I journeyed from my alphabetically-ordered abode to the teeming madhouse next door, carrying Tupperware tubs filled with homemade curries and poppadums, passing a harassed teenage babysitter on her way out. Little King Arthur loves a poppadum: he believes them to be enormous crisps.

I was touched to see the children had cleared – as a detonator clears a derelict building – the dining table and were crashing about with plates. No cutlery, as I have taught them to eat with their hands, in the traditional style. Bethan, their mother, approves of this.

Bethan. Bethan. Where to begin? Bethan is a textile artist. Like most people who describe themselves as 'intensely creative', her house is an unutterable shithole. She creates beautiful fabrics designs that she releases into the world like exquisite doves then returns to a Withnailesque home covered with over-flowing ashtrays and dirty washing. She has rammed cheap Ikea shelves into the rounded crevices of her 17th century cottage (the rampaging Swedes striking again at the soft heart of England) and stuffed them full of pseudo-spiritual clutter (crystals, dream-catchers et al) while her children's plastic detritus is eternally underfoot.

Whenever I visit her about some neighbourly matter, she drags me inside, crying "Claude! Come in! Sit down!" while sweeping several ton of landfill from her exceptionally low sofa. I must sink to its oriental depths, my knees elevated around my ears, to attempt communication: "About the boundary fence –"

We are invariably interrupted by a child's squawks or Bethan will pour forth about her chaotic love life, entirely unfiltered, even if the children are present. Her offspring have weary, wary gazes. They've heard too much.

She once told me she believed in keeping nothing from them.

"Then what have you left to give?" I said. A rather finely turned retort, but she rarely listens. She regards me merely as her usefully retired neighbour: a collector of parcels; a feeder of cats; a sitter of babies.

Guinevere, eavesdropping, once said primly: "Mum says the world's gifts are not hers to give." Insufferable half-baked gap-year philosophy.

"I do hope your mother's not advocating shoplifting," I said.

Bethan smiled tightly. "You're always very interested in how I'm bringing up my children, Claude. What a shame you don't teach anymore."

"I've completed my sentence in the hallowed halls of academia. Forty years of teaching medieval literature was quite enough," I replied.

It's true. Now, aged 65, I write notes for books I will never complete. I make jams. Marmalade.

So, the house next door: intolerable dung-heap. The children: long-haired ragamuffins with differing fathers. The mother: artistic with a romantic weakness for spongers who juggle; prone to mood swings of a normal sort that she labels a bipolar disorder, and, like all attention-seeking narcissists, believes her emotional state is best served by detailing its tedious fluctuations on the internet.

For a self-proclaimed Buddhist, keen to renounce the self, Bethan is impressively committed to online self-promotion. Think for a moment about how one goes about capturing an image of oneself meditating at dawn at Glastonbury Tor. Eyes respectfully closed, with one arm outstretched in the claw-handed Nazi salute of the selfie-taker, sharing her #sacredSomersetspace with her cycloptic iPhone and all her gawping social media 'followers'. Guinevere told me the children are buying a stick for her birthday that will help her take better selfies. Can you even. I just can't.

Bethan wangled my email address from me so I am forced to receive regular message updates, illustrated with numerous Bethan selfies, about her dream to create a 'spiritual wellness centre', most likely in Frome, which she has read in the Saturday supplements is up and coming. Not here, near the motorway just past Bridgwater, a place very much down and spent. How can one fully open one's third eye within spitting distance of the M5? Bethan is lobbying council officials for a house in the Frome area – with attached art/yoga studio.

I am not interested in yoga. Not anymore. I cycle everywhere to keep my blood pressure within medically acceptable levels. The year we lost Michael I cycled from Land's End to John O Groats. "For charity?" asked Bethan. She cannot conceive of doing something for its own sake. Last year she asked me to sponsor her not to drink for a month. A cash reward for a simple act of self-restraint. Recently she asked me to 'support' (oh flattering euphemism) an ascent of Kilimanjaro. A personal challenge, apparently. A subsidised holiday in actuality. She never went. The training became too much.

"No, Bethan, not for charity," I replied. Because there was nothing else to do. Because I had to do something. Because it forced me to sleep.

Anyway. After an enjoyable meal, Arthur, Merlin, Guinevere and I traipsed through their low-ceilinged cottage to the overgrown garden at the rear, the children's medieval costumes – which I bought them last Christmas – dragging behind them. It had rained all week, but that particular September evening was burnished gold. We sat up at the top of the garden, beneath a few ancient apple trees, and we were bathed in glorious sunlight.

Here was the reason Bethan and I chose to live in our conjoined cottages, skulking down a rutted lane on the outskirts of Bridgwater: the view across the Somerset Levels to Glastonbury Tor. Somerset is a stubborn, frustrating and frequently flooded county. Here, on the Levels, it has sunk onto the horizontal, a Dutch flat landscape but for the Tor rising up in the distance. The waters are always rising, keen to make the Tor an island again, and we beleaguered Somersetians must endlessly dredge and drain our soggy homeland. It can be a bit much. But it is the only part of the world I know that offers a view not only across place but through time. It has been called Avalon, Annwn, isle of apples, isle of glass; a place both real and transparent.

When I was a child, after my father died, my mother would drive me from our home in Penrith to my boarding school in Somerset at the start of each new term. We would rattle along in our old Triumph Dolomite, singing hymns – an appropriate musical accompaniment to our journey, which ended with wonderful views across the Vale of Taunton to the Quantock hills. White mist hanging low over the fields. Sunlight shafting through clouds. Mystical Somerset! Resting place of the Holy Grail! I was a romantic boy and believed, on those mornings, I saw England as it truly was: a place of knights and miracles. Perhaps it was merely the accidental conjuring up of a recognisable but wholly fictional place – a storybook illustration. But there it was: Albion. I promised myself I would come back as an adult, when I would have infinite freedom to drive my own cars and read my own books and love my own loves and believe all I wanted to believe.

I keep my promises. A million years later, there I was, all grown up and sitting in a garden with three fancy-dressed children, admiring the autumn sun glinting on the distant watery expanses at Shapwick Heath Nature Reserve. I sometimes take my bike to Shapwick, binoculars hung about my neck, to dally among whitethroats and chiffchaffs, hoping for the rare but rewarding sight of a great white egret. I feel a kinship for this large gangling bird, with its carefully picked-out steps and its supercilious yellow eyes. They're very rarely seen on the Somerset Levels. An enthusiastic volunteer ranger wearing a fleece jacket embroidered with his own name once told me they hope to attract a second bird to form a breeding pair. "The dream we all dream," I murmured into my kagoul.

The children and I were sitting on an old round rug – our version of the Arthurian round table. I had eased my elderly bones into a cross-legged position and handed around my home-made jam tarts, before beginning one of our favourite stories: The Lady of the Lake.

"Did she really live in the lake?" asked Merlin.

"God, you are so dense," exhaled Guinevere, picking at the pastry of her tart. "Cannot even believe for a minute we are any way related."

"Perhaps she was semi-aquatic," I replied.

"Maybe she could sleep underwater," said Merlin.

"And perhaps we will again, Merlin. I read a report in the Bridgwater Mercury that said there are plans to create an inland sea in Somerset."

"Seaside," said Arthur gleefully, clapping his dimpled hands.

It's claimed an inland sea may solve the problem of rising sea levels, which is one of the oft-debated causes of local flooding, but the idea does little to enhance Somerset's appeal with property-buyers, who are unconvinced that letting the water back in is entirely wise. They don't trust it. They fear it has expansionist tendencies. I like to imagine it at night, this new landlocked sea, remembering its origins, the place it came from, and quietly snaking its way back across the county in rivulets and streams and brooks that multiply and intertwine, an underground movement, eventually forming a rising body of water that stretches coast to coast, until ancient Wessex is – with a great earth-crumbling creak – broken away from the mainland, and left to drift off to the horizon.

The children demanded more stories, more stories. I do not allow them to bring their plastic electronica to the round rug so they are itchily frantic for diversionary activities. I tell them of Morgan le Fay – an Arthurian enchantress who lured young knights to their doom, each clanking despondently into her Vale of No Return.

Bethan sees herself as something of a Morgan le Fay. She has been known, after a glass or six of vino cheapo, to attempt moonlit Pagan ceremonies. There are pictures on her kitchen walls of glossy female archetypes in corseted dresses, surrounded by lustily panting wolves. There is, she tells me, a spiritual reason for each of her tattoos. She hurls herself into each new magical enthusiasm for all of a fortnight before dropping it for the next shiny thing, be it auras, yoga or – most entertainingly for the next-door-neighbour with a clear view of her garden – capoeira, a Brazilian art form which combines combat and dance. Fighting oneself in public basically, an activity usually confined to the exceptionally drunk or exceptionally Welsh – one of which often begets the other. (Hush. I was born in Cardiff. I'm allowed. King Arthur himself was also – possibly – a boyo, if he was born at all.)

I find this buffet sampling of other cultures infuriating. But my Michael, I know, would have joined her on the yoga mats. George Harrison was always his favourite Beatle. As a teenager, he'd spent a summer in Goa tantrically tanning in a stamp-sized loin cloth. I have a few photographs of him there – impossibly young. Nineteen. Twenty. How bizarre to see faded Polaroids from the 1960s – that much-mythologised era – and to know we were alive then. Although I was not in Goa. I was in a Durham bedsit, completing my PhD. Hardly Carnaby Street. When my hair reached my collar my landlady made concerned enquiries about the likelihood of me burning 'joss sticks'. She needn't have worried. I burnt only crumpets. Read weighty tomes. Waited for Michael.

He brought back with him a full-body tan and a taste for the food of the Indian subcontinent that I took on from there. Trying to impress him initially I suppose, with my hand-rolled chapattis, but it's an interest that has stayed with me. I even travelled to India for my sixtieth birthday, on one of those organised trips for the socially anxious. People too old or scared to travel alone rounded up and escorted from point of interest to point of interest where carefully vetted 'local spice merchants' were available for awkward conversation.

One day, our autistic little band travelled by air-conditioned minibus to the palm-fringed Anjuna beach Michael had spoken of with such affection. How he would have laughed to see me returning some forty years later with Geoff and Hilda and Clive. It was full of Bethan-a-likes in long skirts dancing on the sand. A great restless meandering of half-naked young people looking for drugs, sex and meaning, like the massing of birds at breeding grounds. Terrible bongos. Michael wasn't there anymore. Of course he wasn't.

I tell the children: "Here's an interesting fact – no need for that face, Guinevere – Morgan le Fay gave her name to the Fata Morgana, a mirage that makes people see castles in the air."

"Whatever," replied Guinevere.

"But which came first, the sorceress or the mist? Do we call the mist Fata Morgana because it reminds us of the story, or was the mist created by Morgan and named in her honour?"

"She's not real," frowned Guinevere.

"But she knew Arthur. And he was a real king," said Merlin.

"He was real but she wasn't," says Guinevere, adjusting her tin foil crown.

"Mum says if Britain is ever in trouble, Arthur will return with the Grail, that's right, isn't it, Uncle Claude?" said Merlin.

"Your mother makes a very strong gin and tonic."

"But you wrote a book about him. He must be real."

"Ah, my favourite wizard. How to explain." My scholarly work: thousands of pages discussing what we politely call 'debated historicity' – the fact that Arthur may never have been. He was – is – an idea that has proved more lasting than any real man. The dark, drinking, singing Celts (and I count myself among them) have clustered on the rocky Western edges of their lands – Wales, Cornwall, Brittany – telling stories of Arthur again and again; twisting a strong rope of words to hand down to those that would come after them. And their desire for those tales to be true was so great, their collective yearning so powerful, that Arthur rose up from the pages of storybooks and entered, triumphant, the pages of history books, his banner flags fluttering.

"Arfur lives there," said Arthur, pointing at the Tor. Presumably he hasn't yet heard his mother's theory that the Tor is a giant earthern breast, constructed by druids to venerate a mighty she-goddess.

"Some believe that the Tor is Arthur's last resting place," I said, stroking his soft head.

"How can he be dead if he's coming back?" asked Merlin.

"It may be that there are different versions of him."

"Like Doctor Who?"

"You should also know that answer is something of a fudge," I added.

"Fudge," whispered Arthur to himself.

"Dead people are just dead," proclaimed Guinevere, the haughty queen.

You know, I've heard Bethan refer to me as a queen. She goes outside to phone her friends, believing erroneously this prevents anyone from over-hearing. She drops it in: "Actually, our next-door-neighbour babysits – this waspish old queen – well, I've never been conventional!"

Waspish, possibly, but not queenly. I've never been showy. I doubt she even means what she says, it's more a way of casually alerting people to the fact she's on first name terms with a gay. We're in high demand out here in the sticks. But my novelty value will only last for so long; I've heard on the grapevine there's a young couple just moved into Chilton Polden, bringing with them wedding rings and adopted twins. Fancy. When Bethan gets wind of Gregor and Tom, I'll be yesterday's news.

It occurs to me – he says lightly, as if he had never thought it before – that it was only an accident of time, an accident of birth, that left me here, washed up alone in this ancient house. If I'd been born thirty years later, the possibility of marriage and kids would have been just that – a possibility. I could have been a father. No. I would have been a father. It's hard not to envy Gregor and Tom. Bill and Paul. Alejandro and Liam.

Michael and I had plans, of course, but only the vague huge-skied ambitions of boys in their twenties: a campervan; a yacht; a house in Andalucía, where we'd stand looped about each other, watching eagles from the terrace. After him, there didn't seem any point in imagining further. But now I have the thought of a family, a home, a hearth. And I have an image of the two of us opening a door, over and over again, to children, our children, becoming teenagers – dragging their holdalls and broken hearts in behind them – teenagers becoming adults becoming parents – *come in, come in, come in* – becoming people who talk about mortgages and traffic, becoming that boring, that busy, that messy, that noisy expanding lineage that is family, family, family.

But anyway. Queenly. The word always puts me in mind of the Queen of Hearts, that shrieker of irrational demands. Is there anything more despised than a barren old queen? The Queen of Hearts, she made some tarts. What else did she do? Oh, nothing. Oh, to be a king.

I mustn't be bitter. Michael would disapprove. He would be popping next door to join Bethan in her hippy tomfoolery. He'd always join in. Make things jolly. He'd help her train for her ascent of Kilimanjaro, and would drag me along too, no doubt. My Michael. My social passport. My link to the world. I would be kinder to her, I think, if he were here. I should be kinder.

I am kind to the children in her stead though. I do that. And it's a treat, not a chore. Their filthy, gap-toothed faces bring me a simple joy that I almost dare not admit to, in case I frighten it away, this rare bird: happiness. How amazingly they are just themselves. How securely they inhabit their bodies. Little Arthur, climbing into my lap, dragging with him the mangled remains of a teddy, so confident of his right to claim this place. And their sudden, furiously urgent hugs. Even Guinevere, usually far above such things.

"See soon," says Arthur, when I carry him to his little train-shaped bed, his head on my shoulder. "See soon."

And as much as I wish I didn't have to watch my neighbour breastfeeding her son when I'm trying to talk about rising damp, I do envy the connection she has with her children. They are of her. I once saw her run towards a wasps' nest Merlin had accidentally disturbed, pick it up and sprint with it, rugby-style, down the garden, to protect him. She told me she didn't feel the stings at all. Bethan, for all her wiki-nonsense, has a passion, a ferocity; a full-hearted immersion in all her ridiculous projects. I have only ever looked on, binoculars round my neck, standing astride my bicycle, one foot on the pedal.

"Arthur must be well bored waiting," says Merlin.

There are many stories of kings in waiting, in many different cultures. Deposed kings, lost kings, issueless kings. The bloodline dries to a halt. The lands turn to ash. The harvests fail. You see where this is going.

I should tell the children they should never – .

No. I shouldn't.

"My turn now," says young Arthur, pulling the tin-foil crown from his sister's head. "My turn."

Guinevere swatted at him then said: "The jam in jam tarts isn't like real jam at all. It's like jelly."

"Jelly and ice-cream," murmured Arthur, lost in a party food reverie.

Merlin bounced a small plastic creature on my knee.

"What's this?" I asked.

"Moshi Monster," he said.

"Wonderful. Is it like the one I saw last week?"

"Different powers."

He placed it tenderly in the palm of my hand. He often brings me things, inscrutable offerings, in the same silent, shy way Bethan's cat brings me dead mice. I find tiny plastic toys carefully balanced on my front gate or tucked into a flower pot on my windowsill, half-buried in the soil, hinged arms upraised.

"You can have it, Uncle Claude. I've got that one. I need a gold one."

"I will treasure it. Will you find a gold one?"

"Maybe. Don't know. A boy at school has one."

"Let's hope so."

He bounced the toy on my palm, twisting it to and fro in a curious folk dance.

"Jam has pips," said Guinevere authoritatively, wiping her mouth with the back of her hand.

Merlin looked up at me then, his dark eyes huge. "Will you live in your house forever, Uncle Claude?"

"I see no reason to leave."

He turned his attention back to the dancing figurine. "We were going to move but we aren't now."

I was startled by a sudden lurch of emotion, like stepping onto a missing stair. "Move?"

"Mum got offered a house in Frome but she said no," he said.

Guinevere continued: "Mum says it's important for us to have a male role model. She says you're not going anywhere, unlike all the other useless bastards she's ever met."

"A role model? She said that?"

"So we will probably stay forever too," said Merlin quietly, nodding, pulling up grass from the lawn.

"Well," I said, and ruffled his hair. "Well, I never. You know, I always thought my future was in modelling."

"That's not what she meant," cried Guinevere, outraged.

"Surely you can see me on the catwalk?"

"Cat," said Arthur, smiling, "walk cat." I reached an arm around him, ducking down to place a swift hidden kiss on his fluffy head.

You can wait for years. You can stand in your immaculately clean kitchen, rolling out your pastry, listening to the clock tick past, and you will realise you keep your house tidy for a dead man because you want him to see how well you've survived when he walks through the door. But in the emptiness of that illogical waiting, that endless vigil, you become a constant, even despite yourself. And perhaps one day, that will prove useful to people you never imagined. Small strange grubby people. Loyalty to an absent cause is still loyalty, after all. We can still recognise it.

"I'm a top model," said Guinevere, holding two jam tarts up to her eyes and sticking her tongue out: a boggle-eyed monster. Her brothers, laughing, scrambled to grab the remaining jam tarts from the tub, so they could hold them up against their own faces and shout: "Uncle Claude! You do it! You do it!"

I took two disintegrating jam tarts and held them up to my eyes and, getting slowly to my feet, gave a great ferocious ear-splitting roar, a sound that boomed and echoed across the Levels, to the Tor, to the sea, sending up a flock of swirling starlings, shaking Arthur in his grave, and the children shrieked, and laughed, and ran.

Caroline Vu

Caroline Vu was born in Vietnam and left her native country at the age of 11. She moved to Canada after spending two years in the US. Caroline's first novel, *Palawan Story* (Deux Voiliers Publishing) won the Canadian Authors Association Fred Kerner Book Award in 2016. That novel was also a finalist for the Quebec Writers' Federation's Concordia University First Book Prize. Her second novel, *That Summer in Provincetown* (Guernica Editions) has been translated into French by Les Editions de la Pleine Lune. Caroline currently works as a family physician in a community health clinic in Montreal.

Television Voices

They think I remember nothing but I remember everything. I remember it too well, our very first day together. Or was it the first week? The first month? The exact date, it doesn't matter anymore. What should I tell them? That you kept me bound in a blanket? That you put me in two grocery bags and hung me on the bathroom doorknob? That I was left hanging there, alone, from morning till dusk? Should they believe this story? No. They wouldn't believe a word of it. Even doubled, the plastic bags would surely rip and I would fall, they'd say. Or the doorknob would give way and my cries would rouse the neighbours' suspicions, they'd tell themselves. How fast they forget me! I wasn't always so well fed and jittery. When they held me for the first time, I weighed less than the two cats on their sofa. My limbs were as limp as the teddy bear they pushed into my face that day. I didn't move then, just as I never moved in our old room.

I remember you waking me each morning. With your right elbow, you rolled me away from your warm body onto the cold floor. There you changed my cloth diaper then washed my face with a wet towel. To my whimpering, you mumbled, "Stop fretting! Am reheating the congee and snake wine now!" You always said the same thing. Those were your only words, day and night. The rice porridge filled my stomach while the snake wine left me quietly content. To that mixture, you always added a sliver of ginger to help me digest. I didn't need more. I never whined for more. Before leaving the room, you'd turn on the old television. You'd leave the volume low enough to bother no one yet high enough to fool me into thinking you were still around. You'd pat my head then you hung me on the doorknob.

Everything I learned, I learned from that colourless television by the kitchen sink. Watching grainy images on a small screen from across the room irritated my eyes. Daily, I shed tears of inflammation as I squinted harder to follow the movement of strangers. Despite my tired eyes, I couldn't ignore that talking machine. It became my addiction. When the snake wine effect wore off, the television voice would kick in. It sang to me, it fed me words you never did. It was reliable so I trusted it. Snuggled inside my bags, I listened and observed intently, absorbing ideas I couldn't quite grasp. Do you remember I hardly grew? Hardly gained weight? Looking like a baby despite my two years of age? Fortunately my brain was spared this stunting. In fact it grew faster than you had ever imagined. With each televised broadcast, my mind expanded and spread. It asked questions I couldn't answer. How are boys different from girls? What makes boys so important? Why are girls left on strangers' doorsteps? Sent away to new families in distant lands? Since you rarely spoke to me, I never learned to verbalize thoughts. The questions in my head remained as voiceless as my yearnings for you.

For two years, I hung double bagged on the bathroom doorknob after you left each morning. For two years, I heard stories of girls being given away and wondered if you would give me away. For two years, I'd ask myself where you went each day, what you did, when would you return to change my diaper. You always came back. Some days you returned after the evening weather forecast. Other days I heard you unlock our door while late night music played on the screen. By that time, darkness had taken over most of our room. Only the television light guided my eyes. Did you know darkness scared me? I hate not being able to see our straw mat on the floor. I thought if I could no longer see it, my place next to you would be lost forever.

On rare occasions, you would come home before sunset. On such days I would notice the marks on your neck – purple circles that would disappear after a few days. I'd wanted to see those marks from close but our dim light bulb hid well your imperfections while the night kept your secrets deeply buried. Your neck marks – one, two, sometimes three – mystified me. They would appear, disappear then reappear at different places. I asked myself what they were. But I should've asked: who did this to you?

Our evening rituals never changed. You would take me down from the doorknob, out of my plastic bags. You would undress me then bring me to the kitchen sink for a quick wash. The cold water always bothered me. I would let out a cry that you'd never register. After dressing me, you would place me on the table, propped up by old cushions. Freed at last from the binding blanket, my arms would attempt a few zigzags in the air. I so wanted to touch your face, to feel the sweat on your skin. But I would always miss my mark and you'd sometimes smile at my awkwardness. I loved these moments. I loved seeing our room from this perspective, meeting your eyes as you turned around to check on me from time to time. Cooking our evening meal gave some lightness to your feet. I remember your humming to the sound of boiling water.

Their talk made no sense to me at first. It sounded nothing like the television voices back home. Their faces – yellow curly hair, big blue eyes, pink cheeks – looked nothing like your black hair, small eyes and sallow skin. Even their smell differed from yours. I did not like the food they fed me — the hard, dry clumps of meat stuck to my throat. Without the snake wine everything became a chore to swallow. But they did not bind me in blankets. Didn't hang me on bathroom doorknobs. Didn't carry me in grocery bags. Free of the constricting blanket, my arms and legs quickly began to move. At first, they only wiggled in the air as I lay on my back like a fallen cockroach. Eventually my limbs learned enough coordination to let me crawl. So I went around the house looking for our old television, our straw mat, our tattered cushions. I searched every day yet found no traces of you anywhere. I saw that the Blue Eyes too, followed me everywhere I went.

My new bed had many soft pillows. It was also full of dolls looking like the Blue Eyes. Yet without warmth, the toys offered no comfort. Sleeping with those stiff and silent plastic babies scared me. Their big staring eyes gave me nightmares. I wanted to turn off the night light to be spared their blue-eyed glare. But my hands had yet to learn that skill. In bed alone, I often thought of you. I missed the noises you made at night. Sometimes you'd scream or sob in your sleep. But most of the time you only breathed regularly. Your snoring reassured me.

The Blue Eyes talked to me constantly. They didn't know I only understood the television language of home. They tried showing me things. Repeated words over and over till my head hurt. The more they said A DOG, A CAT, A BIRD, the more I heard your voice. "Am reheating the congee and snake wine now!" These were the words I carried with me all day.

When I crawled near her feet, the Blue Eyes would bend down to pick me up. She would place me on her lap after removing the two cats from their resting positions. I feared those green-eyed cats as much as I did the plastic babies. Their irises changed colour with the light, glowing in the sun then shutting down at night. This magic trick confused me. I only wanted to see you again, the unwavering darkness of your eyes.

You thought I understood nothing but I understood all. Your unsmiling face, slouched shoulders, silent sigh – told a story so different from the heroic shows I saw on television. From your downcast eyes, I knew neither music nor knowledge graced your weary world. Whatever you did outside our home, you did without conviction, without a flutter of the heart.

I remember you turning off the television as soon as you came home. After washing me, you'd busy yourself with more work – setting traps for mice, sweeping the dusty floor, emptying the bucket of water below the leaking pipe. You had no time for useless activities. The television was only for me.

Some days you made exceptions, leaving the music on. I learned to hate those days for they meant visits from the loud man. I detested his big voice interrupting the quiet of our lives together. How I wished I could cover my ears to protect them from the nonsense shooting out of the man's mouth. But I didn't know how to move my hands in those days. To his usual "money?" you would always nod. Reluctantly you'd take out the coins hidden in a pot to count. You didn't always give him what he wanted. But he never insisted on more. With the snake wine lifting his mood, he'd talk and laugh all night. To his endless chatter, you'd only said "yes", "maybe" or emitted a rare grunt. Whenever the man visited, you'd leave me dangling by the doorknob all evening. I remember you knelt down to feed me as the man looked on, his arms crossed against his chest, his head shaking. In your haste to finish your job, you had forgotten about my soiled diaper. Didn't you know wet dirty diapers caused itchiness and discomfort? You'd answer my cries with some diluted snake wine that you'd feed me spoon by spoon. At bedtime, you'd close the door to shut me out of your sight. Without your hand on mine, without your breath on my back, I imagined all kind of bad omens in the dark. The night turned everything colourless, shapeless, boundary-less – everything except the demons in my head. I hated being made invisible by the lack of light. Do you remember that time the man bumped into me on his way to the toilet? Do you remember his irritation at hearing me cry out in pain? "Useless kid!" he'd screamed. I remember you came running for me. You checked my head and body for bruises. Then you checked the plastic bags for tear. When you found nothing wrong, you returned me to my post by the doorknob. You closed the door but left a light in the bathroom to prevent further collision. My pain subsided and I eventually fell asleep to the smell of urine in the not-yet-flushed toilet.

One day, after watching me crawl unsuccessfully over a cushion, the Blue Eyes got up from her chair. She took my hands in hers, lifted me to a standing position and guided my first few steps toward the bathroom. When I managed to stay erect without falling down, the Blue Eyes kissed my head. The other Blue Eyes laughed upon seeing this feat. Immediately he fetched his camera and began recording my unsteady walk. That whole afternoon was spent taking photos to fill the many empty pages of my baby album.

You didn't have a camera at home but they did at the orphanage. Do you remember bringing me there? I do. It was the first time I left our room. New sensations overwhelmed me the minute we stepped outside. The pleasure of breezes, the acrid odour of congestion left me disoriented. In our hot, overcrowded tram, my stomach turned. You grimaced when I vomited on you. To prevent new accidents, you wrapped a plastic bag around my mouth and held it tightly there. When we got off the tram, you seemed confused by the many street signs. On the sidewalk, you stopped random strangers to ask for directions. Then you ran for cover as heavy rain poured down on us. I heard you laugh for the first time when you saw the accumulated water in my plastic bags streaming out of a hole at the bottom. Yes, we were wet, very wet. Inside a big white house someone asked, "How old?" To my surprise, you replied, "Eight months." You also surprised me with your many kisses on my cheeks. You parted my wet hair and whispered in my ear. "Mei, Mei, Mei…" you repeated over and over. When you handed me to an ugly old woman in white, I howled in protest. I shook violently but you couldn't see. You'd already left without turning back. The old woman sang me a song while changing my clothes. Then she waved goodbye after putting me in a crib with two other crying babies.

At the orphanage, they took photos of us every month. I remember the flashing light bothering my eyes and I wondered why people smiled for these tiresome occasions. The old woman kept a set of clean clothes for our photo sessions. We were also given new toys to hold during the duration of the shoot. We knew we could only pose with the toys in our hands. Playing with them or breaking them would earn us an immediate scold. To keep us happy and smiling the old woman promised us a candy each at the end of the photo shoot. Excited, many of us did smile or laugh for those photos. I smiled a few times too.

The Blue Eyes showed me my orphanage photos not long after I arrived at their house. Repeatedly they pointed to me, then to the images of me on their kitchen walls. They liked using simple gestures, thinking of me as a mindless, speechless doll.

The Blue Eyes owned a large television set. But no voices emanated from it. Most of the time it stayed dark and silent in the main room. Only on special occasions did they turn it on. The Blue Eyes liked watching films of their cats. They'd also laughed at their television selves blowing candles, cutting cake and singing on screen. When images of me appeared, they'd suddenly become quiet. Then they'd pick me up to pat my head and play with my hair. The Blue Eyes always smiled when braiding my straight black hair.

It was not long before I learned to climb the stairs by myself. The Blue Eyes marvelled at the speed of my development. They took pictures of my wandering everyday. Nobody had told them my true age. My small frame and lack of language had fooled them. They mistook me for a toddler, when at four, my mind already understood a television dialect intended for the mass. The more the Blue Eyes shower me with their words, the more deaf and dumb I become. I do not want to hear their "Good girl!" I'd rather hear your "Stop fretting!" I'd rather hear the language of our television telling me tales of baby girls left out in the cold. I wonder what happened to those girls? I wonder if you still remember me?

Barbara Weeks

Barbara Weeks is a writer, teacher and former journalist. She has an MA in Creative Writing and was runner–up in both the Jerwood Historical Short Story competition and Wells Festival of Literature Short Story Competition. Her work has been selected for various competition longlists and shortlists, including BBC Radio 4 Opening Lines. She has taught Creative Writing in community education and is currently an ESOL tutor working with refugees. Barbara has two adult sons and lives in West Wales with her dog, Fi.

Rollerama

'Run,' she says, 'take my hand,' and so I take it and run with her, tripping over laces, untied. We run from the Rollerama past the Methodist Chapel, along unlit alleyways, backyards and outside bogs; graffiti on a wall – *Maggie Thatcher rot in hell*.

We cross the river bridge and keep running until we get to the playground, dark and overshadowed by tower blocks and the junkyard behind; a bonfire of scaffolding poles and stolen cars dredged from the river. Breathless, we sit on the swings, wrap our arms around the cold chains, and link fingers again.

'I broke my arm once, fell off the slide,' she says. The slide, like the swings, has rusted, paint brittle and flaking. Grass sprouts through cracks and puddles where the frames embed in the concrete.

'I feel weird,' I say.

'Weird or wired?'

'Just weird.'

She rummages in her knapsack, tosses a Satsuma to me.

'Vit C, bring you down a bit,' she says.

She knows these things I think, so I break the skin, citrus sweet and sticky, peel off segments, feel weird still.

'I'd forgotten I could roller skate,' I say.

She gives me a look, wicked-like.

'Ha, ha,' I say and eat another segment, and then another.

I should tie my laces.

We'd walked up Garth Mountain the previous week, skived off school. It rained all day, feet soaked, staring at the grass. I didn't know what I was looking for, just followed her lead, picking slippery little mushrooms from between stones and weeds, tossing them in to a sandwich box. Afterwards, back in town, we went to '*Crisp'n'Fry,*' fingers grubby from the mountain and the greasy newsprint. Salt and vinegar steamed from the hot chips and made our mouths and eyes water. The taste of it on her lips when she kissed me.

'Next week?' she'd said as we'd parted at the corner of my street. 'Rollerama?' and I'd watched her go, hair wet from the rain, vinegar kisses on my lips and felt as though we'd shared the greatest secret there ever was.

'Better?'

I've eaten three of them, satsumas.

I shrug. Cold and damp. The wind coming up the river brings the sea with it, ruffles washing on the balconies of the towers like feathers on a giant black bird.

'Bloody school stuff... hate it... don't you?' she says.

I do. Teeth chattering. I'll find the words in a minute.

'Twats, they are.'

I nod. Twats.

'Thought it would be a laugh, didn't mean to freak you out or nothing.'

'It's alright,' I say. I've found some words, but they are the wrong ones.

Earlier, on Taff Embankment, we'd sat on a bench, across the river from the brewery, chewed on the mushrooms and washed them down with cider. Sharp, fizzing, it ran from the corners of our mouths and down our necks, inside our coats and t-shirts, made us shiver. She pulled me close, to keep me warm.

'C'mon,' she said, 'it'll be a laugh.'

I just wanted to sit there with her, cold and weird, breathing air thick with the stink of the river and stewing hops. Didn't need anything more than the black sky, belladonna creeping down the embankment, her arms round me.

'I dunno,' I said.

But she slipped her hand in mine; led me astray.

To the Rollerama. School thing. Pop and crisps and all that.

'You coming in?' One of the teachers spotted us, but I'd changed my mind and looked at her, thinking no, bad idea; cider for blood and the mountain lifting us from our feet. I pushed my hands in my pockets but she grabbed my sleeve, pulled me forward.

'Come, on, it'll be a laugh,' she said again.

The teacher gave us roller-skates and we sat on cold plastic chairs, pushed our stuff under a table. The disco ball splattered colour, like paint flicked from a brush, as girls with big hair and ra-ra skirts circled the parquet floor and boys tried to bump in to them, grab their tits. We laced on the skates and stood, legs shaking as we crossed the strips of light on the floor, wading through music that hissed as if being strained through a sieve: all *Human League* and *Tin Drum*.

She took my hand, drew me forward – as if it was ok for us to hold hands – and we drifted, glided, wobbled and stumbled; roller-skates with their own will, their own purpose. I found my balance, pulled away, left her behind and she chased me, weaving between tutting girls and boys with bad haircuts and baggy trousers. Going faster, not because we knew how to skate or knew what we were doing, but because that's what happens when you find your feet; you keep going and you go faster and faster until you stop.

And I let her catch me again, fingers locked.

'Torvill and Dean!' she said, and kissed me and I thought, yeah, easy, so easy, let's go, let's do it; cider for blood and wings on my skates. And I held her hand tight and she spun me, round and round, wound up like a lasso. Round and round, wheels clattering madly. Round and round until I hit something; skin and bones, big hair, big mouth. It fell to the ground and started to wail like a wounded animal; girl, floor, crying.

I looked down at her, at the ra-ra skirt and shiny lips, a queen bitch, crumpled on the parquet, her friends outraged and keening as if she were a dying swan.

'Fucking cows, what d'you do that for? ' someone said.

'Fucking weirdos!'

'Fucking slags, you're fucking sick you are…'

But it didn't matter what they said; I felt a hand on my shoulder, a whisper in my ear:

'Told you it would be a laugh,' her breath sweet and wicked, and she began to laugh, loud and careless. And if she's laughing, I thought, it must be funny, so I laughed too, laughed so hard it hurt like a punch in the guts. Laughed until I thought I'd wet myself.

'What's wrong with you? What you laughing at? Coulda bust her leg or something. Coulda killed her,' the twats said, helping their queen up from the floor, words running away from them like the wheels on the skates that rattled and spun; unstoppable. .

And they crowded in on us as the lights from the disco ball crawled up the walls and the room spun and rolled and we laughed. And even as she pulled me away and our legs tangled with the roller-skates, we kept laughing. Even as we stumbled to the cold plastic chairs, pushed and spun by the twats, we kept rolling. Even as we pulled on our daps and grabbed our stuff, we were still spinning, still flying. Roller – bloody – rama!

'I feel sick,' I said.

'Fucking lezzas,' they said.

'Run!' she said.

I brush the satsuma peel from my lap to the concrete and kick it away as we swing. I still feel weird and my skin is sticky with cider and satsuma. And she's restless, stands on the swing, stretches up to the top bar and sways for a moment, twisting her legs in the chains.

'I can see the mountain from here,' she says.

Looking at her makes me dizzy, and I want to tell her not to fall and break her arm; you can see the mountain from anywhere. But she is casting around. Has ideas.

'Over there!' she says and drops from the frame and leads me across to the junkyard, like a monkey climbing the catch-fencing, landing on scaffolding poles and car doors.

'Look at this!' She's found an old shopping trolley and breaks it free, pushes it up and over the top of the fence, metal snagging on metal. It drops, crashes on the ground; she follows, landing soft as if in slippers. She sets the trolley upright, checks the wheels, rolls it back and forth , like she knows what she's doing.

'Get in!'

'What me?'

'Yeah, you!' she says.

'What for?'

'Why not?'

'It'll be a laugh,' I say, before she does.

I climb in, wipe my sticky hands on my jeans and hold my knees tight and she leans over, kisses me, citrus lips. I see my daps, laces undone, and think I should tie them but she's pushing already, running along the path that circles the playground. Riding shotgun she steers the trolley as it shakes over potholes and ruts, the playground on one side and the dark track of the river on the other. She pushes, she runs, skids to a halt. I hit my head on the side, still trying to tie my laces, and I say:

'Again! Again!' as if I'm still a kid and my secret is still inside me, not running free with her.

'Rollerama!' she says and her voice bends in the wind as we go faster, shake harder. 'It's like a giant bloody roller skate!' And I look at her, laughing, and think I love her, imagine that it will always be like this: night-time, a playground, just me and her.

We slide to a stop near the junkyard gate and my eyes stay fixed on her.

'Shit.'

I turn, follow to where she looks.

Coming across the playground – big hair and ra-ra skirts, bad haircuts and baggy trousers; twats.

She turns the trolley around.

'Let me out!' I say and try to climb but she is pushing, running, can't hear me over the thud of chasing footfall and the rattle of wheels on concrete.

'It's alright,' she says, but we are disappearing into blackness, closer to the edge of the world where it fades into wasteland, where the path becomes a pile of stones bound with ragwort and rubbish, where the river stretches itself and becomes the bay.

They are shouting: 'Fucking dykes...' and I try to stand, but I am caged, laces snagged in the wire mesh.

'It's alright,' she says again; she knows these things, she falls from swings and climbs fences and conquers mountains.

Vit C brings you down a bit.

She said it would be a laugh.

So I sit down, but the trolley tips onto the black grass and down the bank, sliding to the river where it flows from the city, from the Rollerama to the junkyard, to catch us as we fall. I taste water thick with coal dust and run-off from the brewery, washing the citrus from my lips. Shadows on the path – people, towers, swings and slides and the mountain that frames the city, all vanish.

The river floods the space between my skin and my clothes, fills my socks, and I kick my daps from my feet. I rise up as the trolley sinks, twisting and turning and she does the same, wide eyed, hair black, as if swimming in oil. Like water-babies we are, arms out, reaching; take my hand.

She pulls the knapsack from her back, fruit in the water, a can of spray paint – *Maggie Thatcher rot in hell* – and tries to swim. But she is a tangle and a jumble and that arm, broken again, is twisted and odd. She is lifted and bobbed like flotsam out into the bay and I try to call to her, I'll find the words in a minute, but water fills my mouth as I fight with the tide.

I feel weird.

She's at the end of my road, eating chips. Every evening after school she sits beneath the street light so she knows that I can see her. Her arm has been in plaster for weeks.

I can still feel coal and silt in my hair when I run my fingers through. I still feel dizzy from the cider and the runaway wheels. I can still taste the vinegar from her kiss on my lips.

But they watch me now, everyone. Parents. Teachers Twats. Maggie Thatcher.

I am a strange thing.

And they keep me inside.

To keep me safe from myself.

And her.

After school, after tea, I go to my bedroom and turn on the light. I put a record on the turntable and pull the curtains back so she can see me and I twist and turn, a dancing shadow; *Human League and Tin Drum.* I dance like I am on wheels, spinning and turning as if I can out-spin the world, spin faster than time so that I can reach into a future where I can be me.

Me and her.

Because she knows these things; these feelings.

Spin and spin and spin and spin.

Roller- bloody-rama!

Charlotte Wührer

Charlotte Wührer is a Berlin-based writer and translator from Newcastle-under-Lyme, England. She trained as a primary school teacher before going on to study for a MA in English Studies at the Free University, Berlin. In 2016, she was shortlisted for *The Reader Berlin*'s Summer Short Fiction Competition, and longlisted for *Mslexia*'s Children's Novel Competition. Charlotte is published in Issue 15 of *SAND Literary Journal*, in *FU Review* and *Berlin Unspoken*. She can be found online at *Potluck Mag* and *Leopardskin and Limes*, and she writes for Berlin's *Daddy Mag*.

Minor Reports

The house swarms with Quentin's students. The women, if they can be called that, are the worst, looking at and touching everything. They run their fingers over the furniture. When they come to me they take stock impassively. Their eyes flick over me from top to bottom, like a barcode scanner. I find, oddly, that they all look a little like cats. They wear a uniform of black kohl flicks on their unwrinkled eyelids, which curve up hopefully towards their eyebrows. "This is a woman," I imagine throwing up my hands to say.

Quentin comes in with a tray of drinks and stops short, as if he hadn't expected me to be home. But where else would I be? "Ah," he says, "and this is the woman I live with." The students nod without much interest and take a drink. I am not offered one, so I turn, with a flush crawling up my chest towards my face, to pull and prod at the books on the shelf behind me until their spines line up seamlessly.

It is colder today than it should be, given it is the first day of spring. When Quentin is driving to work the raindrops on his windscreen are slushy, at that tipping point between sleet and snow.

"The daffodils will suffer if the cold spell doesn't break soon," he says prophetically when he returns, and I suppose I must believe him when he tells me that they have been lining the roads for weeks already, their yellow heads all looking the same way: down at the ground, like lonely little people scuffing their feet. Quentin brings these minor reports from outside. On good days I swallow everything he offers greedily, and on the bad I don't believe a word. He says, "Turn on the television if you're bored," but one thing I have vowed not to do is precisely that. I suppose my reasons are comparable to those which bestselling authors have for not reading reviews of their second novels.

As I am having lunch the cat brings in a mouse, still alive, and they play until it is dead. When it is over there is only a bloody kidney left under the kitchen table. Clever cat.

I am at that stage of my life where it ought not to matter so much. Quentin says if I were twenty years younger I could do worse than kill myself, in my situation. I paraphrase. What he actually says is that if he were in my position he would kill himself, twenty years neither here nor there. He says it very mildly, with his back to me as he does something prosaic and homely. I forget what. Perhaps he shakes out a new bin bag and hooks it over the rim of the kitchen bin. As it is, no one is killing themselves or anybody else. Instead we are thinking of leaving the country, which is less dramatic but still a kind of death. Quentin, at least, has ties in France, and he speaks a little French.

It ought not matter much, and perhaps it really does not. The initial shock has been dealt with. The fabric of life is still the same. There are things to be done in the garden, a thought which brings a glimmer to the day when I think it.

The first time I leave the house after I am arrested and then released on bail, I go to work. Not actually to perform the duties associated with my work, but to sever once and for all the ties forged in almost three decades at the same establishment. To go to work in the traditional sense is an impossibility. My desktop computer has been confiscated, along with my personal laptop and my phone.

Human Resources calls the landline on a Wednesday to summon me for the Friday. Quentin is out and I do not tell him. On the way, naked tree branches whip at the top and sides of the double-decker bus I am sitting on. The sound rips through the space like gunshots, which is what I thought the first one was. I pull the bag on my lap into me, as if the soft canvas of it could stop a bullet. Some of the branches sound not like wood but metal on glass, and everyone on the bus cringes, teeth bared like dogs.

"Just because you're paranoid," Quentin used to say, "doesn't mean they're not out to get you." He's not said it for a while, and I know that if he were sitting next to me he would watch me flinch and stay silent. Not least because yesterday's report from the outside included actual gunshots and death on Westminster Bridge. It feels more like an accident than a miracle that we're still alive.

I keep my head down. I have a fear that I will see someone I know and they will ask me where I have been. It is not an irrational fear. It is a real one, based on an event which will happen. I have dreamed it, a prophetic dream. When I woke up afterwards the base of my spine tingled in that way it does. In it I was jogging along the towpath by the canal, and the blood popping in my legs felt like cellulite pockets exploding. I ran flat-footed and splattered mud gleefully up my shins.

"Hi! Hiya! It's you! I thought it was you!" A hand grabbed me by the forearm. "Where have you been?" A diminutive woman with hennaed hair braided into two diminutive plaits pulled me to the side of the towpath.

"It's not," I said, and I shrugged my arm free. "You have the wrong person." The diminutive woman was Sarah from the bookclub, and she said my name like a question, peering myopically into my face. I shook my head and feigned bewilderment. An elderly man with her face who I took to be her father stood at her side, but we both ignored him. Sarah and I looked at one another for a few seconds longer, and then I carried on down the towpath with both their eyes following me.

The woman in the HR office is what Quentin would call a cool customer. She is what I would call streamlined. She has not a single excessive flap of fabric or gram of fat on her person. She is wearing owlish glasses with thick tortoiseshell frames, which draw attention to her high cheekbones and the hollows below them. Her straight long hair is pulled into a ponytail like a waterfall; I would like to run it through my fist, from top to bottom. It swings when she turns her head to look at me standing in her door, my fingers raised to rap at it even though it is open. She stands to shake my hand with surprising force for such thin fingers, and then she sits, waiting for me to speak first. The look she gives me is inscrutable. I go back to the ponytail and pretend I have it in my hand.

Eventually one of us has to say something, and it will not be me. She clears her throat and says:

"So."

Her look might be inscrutable, but there is a whole world in the "so". It contains all of the people who know me, and all of the people who don't know me but have recently read about me in the newspapers and think that they know me. Everyone in that world is talking about me at the same time. The "so" is so loud that I can't speak myself. I worry that if I do it will come out as shouting, as it apparently does when I am listening to my music on my headphones and trying to talk at the same time.

No matter that Quentin says there has been nothing in the newspapers yet, I can't believe that.

"Not until the trial," he adds, a little cruelly.

I am not a shouter. I am meek and mild and this is why everyone, all the people in this world of that "so", are surprised. If it were quieter I would tell the HR woman my story. Being meek and mild is what has put me here in her chair, and I can join up all the dots in a way that she would probably understand.

I still have some of the old need to be liked – it is a curse – so after she says "so" and the people of its world have had their say and quietened down, I say I am not sure why I am sitting there in her office. How can I help her?

She tells me she knows things must be uncomfortable for me, and that they will be getting more so when the whole thing goes to court. "How can I help *you*?" she asks. I am surprised by the straightforwardness of the word "court", and think she has probably said it by accident. It's not difficult to catch the real sense of her words. By "I" she means "we", which for me means "them". This puts me on the wrong, lonely side of the equation. And when she says things will become more uncomfortable, she means shit will hit the fan.

By "help" she means "cutting the umbilical cord".

I stay silent.

She says, "Let me put it another way. In an ideal world we would not be dealing with journalists," and she stands up before she has finished the sentence. I stand up in sympathy, and then realize that it means our meeting is over.

"In an ideal world" – I mull that over.

I watch Quentin's lips when he brings me a cup of tea to the bed. He does this every morning before he leaves for work. More often than not they are pressed into a thin, anxious line. In the beginning he did not look at me. Now sometimes he smiles. There is no guarantee that when he returns I will have drunk the tea. Often it is right there where he left it, a viscous film building on the surface of the liquid, all the white of the milk slowly pulling and pooling together as if for safety.

I have become somewhat devil-may-care. Some days I lie there next to the tea and consider my options. Some days I don't think about anything much and enjoy not being at work. On these days the idea of the garden flickers on and off on the horizon, and the sky grows a little bigger, opening the ribs of itself before collapsing again. Usually to coincide with Quentin's homecoming. He often greets me with a countdown. Four weeks until the trial. Three weeks. Fifteen days. Inevitably a letter comes to push back the day and it starts all over again. Seven weeks. Four weeks.

On other days I am so sorry that I call him at work. I pretend to crave a particular food for him to buy before he comes home.

As I'm waiting, Lily, our daughter, comes for her boxes of books, which is the last of her to leave. The good thing to come of everything is the money, which has paid for her house. She is young, and does not know that the whole of life is growing older but not up.

"Mum," she says, "God, get up."

No, I think, not up. I am going the other way: I am on an unstoppable downward trajectory. I could get up and run and the past would snowball along behind me, picking up every bit of the detritus of my life, every misdeed and mistake, every thought-crime and half-baked intention. The snowball would grow and grow until there is no sky left to be seen, and then it would swallow me. Woman down! So I will not get up.

Lily comes on a down day, a day on which the snowball is no more than a hair's breadth behind me. I am lying next to the tea considering my options, and the sound is of rumbling and imminent burial.

She had been in the house when the police came. "Paedophile," one of them had spat at me.

I do get up then, in body not in spirit, and find another mouse in the kitchen. It presses itself into the skirting board, which is the same shade of brown as itself, and quiveringly makes itself as small as it can. Lily has followed me from the bedroom. I feel caught out, like a clown without make-up. "Cat," I say, rubbing the hard bit of skull between its eyes, "well done." Lily tells me I am sick and piles up the boxes at the back door through which she had entered. It is still open. Outside there is a car with the engine running. She places boxes into its boot: one, two, three of them. There is a shape at the steering wheel and she climbs in next to it without looking back at the house or at me.

Half hours trickle away. I move around the house picking things up and putting them back down again, not knowing where to wait. An aeon later Quentin returns. He is joyful and kisses me on the lips for what I think is the first time.

He starts breathlessly. He was on the train to London in the toilets, and after the door slides shut and locks a jovial pre-recorded voice lists all the things passengers are not allowed to flush: nappies, sanitary towels, paper towels. There are hailstones in his hair, and he leaves almost black, wet footprints on the tiles when he walks through the kitchen in his socks

I am greedy, greedy, greedy, overwhelmed suddenly by a voracious, bottomless feeling a little like how I imagine the hunger of starvation must feel – I do not want him to stop listing unflushable things.

"Gum, old phones, junk mail. Hopes. Dreams. Goldfish." He stops to laugh and with that his story is over. I have to say I am not sure what the point is, but I am still ravenous. And I do like a good list. What do his dreams look like to him, I wonder? To me they look like the flickering of eyeballs behind his almost translucent eyelids, which leaves a little too much to the imagination. In the early days we often shared our dreams.

I swallow my hunger and tell him in a measured voice that I don't like him going to London with the capital in lock-down.

"Well, what can we do?" he says. I worry that I'm not laughing, but I can't fake it anymore; another thing to have come of all this. He's still smiling as he fills the space with his quiet movements. There is something merciful about this dance of his. "Life goes on," he says, pseudo-philosophically. And then he says it again, because the second time he has realized the dark relevance of the words to our situation, and wants me to know it. I grit my teeth. Sometimes he can't help himself.

A long silence. "Or, stay here with me," I say, trying it for size, pretending we say these things. But he does not hear, or pretends not to.

More half hours trickle away. The lights are turned on and the smell of baking bread, which is his domain, drifts through the house. When Quentin takes the bin bag out in the dusk he finds a badger rearing up on its hind legs in front of the wheelie bin. It is muscular and almost eclipses the sickle moon. He drops the bag and runs back into the kitchen. When he tells me I laugh, thinking it is the funny kind of report again, better late than never.

But I get it wrong. He is panting and grim-lipped. He snarls, like a badger himself, that I should go out and see for myself if I don't believe him. I believe him.

"I believe you," I say, grovelling. My voice sounds fake and sycophantic even to my own ears. And shrill, whole octaves too high. A moment of bright white clarity courses through me hotly, leaving a prickle of sweat on my upper lip which I don't wipe off on purpose. The feeling of it reminds me of the game I used to play with Lily, where we would eat doughnuts without letting ourselves lick the sugar from our lips. The bright white clarity clears the fog which settles in my head from so much waiting and being indoors. France is a dream; the garden is a dream. Human Resources and pooling milk and rage and gunshots and guilt and badgers and fear are the reality, but the most real and worst thing of all is knowing that the worst thing has not yet happened. There is no way of knowing when or what that will be. Maybe this is it. It is impossible to tell.

"Hey," I say, "Hey!" Quentin has taken his jacket from the back of a chair, and is putting it on. "I said I believe you," I tell him loudly, placing myself in front of him so that he has to look at me. "You can't go," I tell him firmly, taking his face between my hands and hoping for him to soften at the shoulders.

He sets them firmly and squarely against me, peels my fingers gently from his face and vanishes into the dark.

I find another bloody, inedible organ on the kitchen floor and scoop it up with a square of kitchen paper. "Clever cat," I say, with my heart not in it, and go back to waiting.

Judges' Profiles

Tania Hershman (Chair)

Tania Hershman is the author of three celebrated short story collections: *Some of Us Glow More Than Others* (Unthank Books, 2017), *My Mother Was An Upright Piano: Fictions* (Tangent Books, 2012), and *The White Road and Other Stories* (Salt, 2008) and co-author of *Writing Short Stories: A Writers' & Artists' Companion* (Bloomsbury, 2014). Her debut poetry collection, *Terms and Conditions (Nine Arches Press)* was published in the summer of 2017. Tania's short stories and poetry have been widely published and broadcast on BBC Radio 3 and 4. She is curator of ShortStops (www.shortstops.info), celebrating short story activity across the UK & Ireland, a Royal Literary Fund fellow at Bristol University and is completing a PhD in Creative Writing at Bath Spa University. www.taniahershman.com

Roshi Fernando

Roshi Fernando is the winner of the 2009 Impress Prize and the author of the acclaimed short story collection, *Homesick* (Bloomsbury). She has a PhD in Creative Writing and lectures on short stories. She was shortlisted for the 2011 *Sunday Times* EFG Short Story Award and longlisted for the Frank O'Connor International Short Story Prize in the same year.

Simon Key

Simon Key is the co-owner of the award winning Big Green Bookshop in Wood Green, North London. He opened the shop in 2008, with his business partner Tim West, after the big chain store where they worked in Wood Green closed, leaving the area with no dedicated bookshop. Simon has worked in bookshops since he left school, starting in Bristol's legendary George's Bookshop in Park Street. He moved to London, and spent many years working in various Waterstones, including Charing Cross Road, Notting Hill and Oxford Street. Since opening the Big Green Bookshop, Simon has championed the short story and the shop not only has a dedicated short story book group, it also holds regular events, with guests including Will Self, Sophie Hannah, Magnus Mills and previous Bristol Prize judge Nikesh Shukla. Simon's new publishing company, Timeline Books, has also recently published a brilliant collection of short stories by Joseph D'Lacey called *Splinters*. @Biggreenbooks

Juliet Pickering

Juliet Pickering is a literary agent at Blake Friedmann Agency, representing a wide range of fiction and non-fiction writers. She represents short story writers Janice Galloway, Anneliese Mackintosh and Benjamin Johncock, and novelists Kerry Hudson and Sue Moorcroft – in fact, all of them have written both long and shorter stories! Juliet is a BIG Shirley Jackson fan, and also loves the short fiction of George Saunders, Dan Rhodes, Roald Dahl and Daphne Du Maurier.

Acknowledgments

We are so grateful to the wonderful people below whose generous work and contributions to this year's competition have made it such a great experience:

The judging panel – Tania Hershman (chair), Roshi Fernando, Simon Key, Juliet Pickering; our readers – Diane Becker, Imogen Cheetham, Lucy Cowie, Jo Darque, Fran Ham, Katherine Hanks, Lu Hersey, Alice Jones, Richard Jones, Mike Manson, Bertel Martin, Eleanor Pender, Dawn Pomroy, Pam Smallwood, Berni Vinton and Megan Vowles. Chris Hill, Jonathan Ward, Harry Sussams and the 3rd year Illustration students at University of the West of England. Tangent Books; Kathy McDermott, Polly Ho-Yen and Bristol Libraries; Peter Morgan and Mark Furneval at ScreenBeetle; Bristol 24/7; Jane Guy and The Bristol Hotel. And Lon Barfield, Joe Burt, Annette Chown, Nicky Coates, Andy Hamilton, Sylvie Kruiniger, Marc Leverton, Natasha Melia, Dave Oakley, and Thomas Rasche.

And a huge thank you to all the writers who submitted such brilliant stories and who always provide us with so much captivating reading.

2017
Bristol Short Story Prize
Longlist

Ghusl – Dima Alzayat

Jigsaw Wabi Sabi – David Brennan

Road Trips and Fairy Tales – Emily Brewin

A Place Called Out – Clementine Ewokolo Burnley

How to Curate a Life – Rachel Connor

Between a Rock and a Hard Place – Seonaid Cook

Voltage – Paul Duffy

The Prickly Pears – Amber Duivenvoorden

Saving Riona – Tanya Farelly

New Skin – Laurie Frankel

All the Names for Animals – Bryan Fulton

Missing Days – Rebecca Gabay

The End of Eternity – Kay Gillard

The House Not Far from Time – Marlene Hanna

ESO 378 Nebula – Jennifer Harvey

Big Secrets Everybody Knows – Conor Houghton

Born from Red – Stephanie Hutton

They Even Painted Over Dead Flies – Kate L Jefford

Autumn Colours – James Kennedy

Glassblower's Lung – Louise Kramskoy

Lucky – Laura Long

The Land of the Pretty – Anita MacCallum

Wealth of Nations – Chetna Maroo

Wednesdays – Rebecca Miller

Things – Amanda O'Callaghan

Skyward! – Poppy O'Neill

Things Carried Over – Bunmi Ogunsiji

The Cows Are Out for Spring – Grace Palmer

The Lost Kings of Somerset – Joanna Quinn

When We Were Nothing But Motion – Julie Reverb

Winter Solstice – Margaret Ries

That Moment – Ayesha Manazir Siddiqi

When You Are Hiding from What it Means to Be a Person – Taymour Soomro

Orange – Rachel Stoeter

Private View – Carina Swantee

The World Gravitates Towards the Ditch – Meg Tuite

Television Voices – Caroline Vu

Rollerama – Barbara Weeks

Minor Reports – Charlotte Wuehrer

This is All Mostly True – withdrawn 11/07/2017. Writer's name withheld so as not to compromise another competition.

Notable Contenders

Swan Song – Abigail Ashley

Ce Soir – Honoria Beirne

Bionic Girl – Mara Blazic

The Other Woman – Emma Franieczek

Romeo – Nada Holland

My Coronation Year – Elin Howe

The Color – B.A. Jones

The Woodcutter's Wife – Sara Kellow

The Darkness Behind the Walls – Lyndsey Seaborn

The Shape of Things – Richard Snow

The Leopard Priest – Alex Valk